THE WOMAN IN THE CELLAR

They are downstairs. Assembled. Standing at the foot of the stairs. Peggy and Darlin' holding hands. Brian with his mouth agape. Brian has been the first one down, all excited. As they crossed the lawn he asked, watcha got in there, dad? A mountain lion? He was kidding of course and Cleek had acknowledged the fact with a grin. A hellova lot more interesting than a mountain lion, son, he said. So now Brian stands there beside him. And his father is right. This is much more interesting than any cat . . .

Other books by Jack Ketchum:

JOYRIDE
COVER
OLD FLAMES
TRIAGE (anthology)
OFFSPRING
OFF SEASON
THE GIRL NEXT DOOR
SHE WAKES
PEACEABLE KINGDOM
RED
THE LOST

JACK KETCHUM
&
LUCKY MCKEE

THE WOMAN

Dorchester
Publishing

DORCHESTER PUBLISHING

May 2011

Published by

Dorchester Publishing Co., Inc.
200 Madison Avenue
New York, NY 10016

ISBN 13: 978-1-4285-1114-9

The "DP" logo is the property of Dorchester Publishing Co., Inc.

Printed in the United States of America.

Visit us online at www.dorchesterpub.com.

ACKNOWLEDGMENTS

From Ketchum:

Thanks to Andrew, Bill and my partner Lucky. To Brauna for the dream. To Paula for damn near everything. To Kristy—she knows perfectly well why. And to Pollyanna for direct and terrible inspiration.

From McKee:

To Ma and Pa for rearin' me right, my sisters Boog, Jaye, and Angie for being great women, my brothers Kevin and Chris for not being like Cleek, and my partners in crime, Andrew, Bill and Polly. And to you, Dallas, for showing a kid how it's done.

CONTENTS

THE WOMAN

"You want to kiss her. I want to taste her. It's just the same."
—Issei Sagawa

"In every dream home
A nightmare"
—Joe Jackson

"I talked to god last night. She says that if she can ever get her cunt sufficiently clean again, she just might forgive you ignorant pricks who raped her."
—Jerzy Livingston, The Stroup Stories

PART ONE

ONE

The Woman has no concept of beauty.

She herself is not beautiful. Not unless power is beauty, because she is powerful, over six feet tall, with long arms and legs, almost simian in their lean strength. But her wide gray eyes are empty when they are not watchful and she is pale from lack of light, filthy, parasite and insect bitten and smelling of blood like a vulture. A wide smooth scar runs from just below her full right breast to just above her hip where eleven summers ago a shotgun blast had peeled her flesh away. Over her left eye and extending beyond her ear a second blast has left another scar. Neither her eyebrow nor her hair from forehead to the back of her ear has ever grown again.

She looks as though struck by lightning.

The Woman is not beautiful, and has no concept of beauty . . .

It is nearly dawn, the darkest hour behind her now and she has left the deep forest and the hardpack rocky trails she has walked for hours, for days perhaps, the fever bright within her, night to day and back again perhaps, all these trails so well-known to her, for the beach at last. She is exposed here in the dawning but she has stopped and listened along the way and doubled back time and again so she is certain she is not pursued. They have given up.

If they have ever followed her at all in the dark. She has moved only in the dark.

Her wounds are graced with fortune—so close together this time at her left side. The knife and the bullet. The crescent moon and the full moon mere inches apart. She has staunched them with mud and wrapped them tightly with her belt. There will be little blood trail for them to follow.

Still, she must heal.

There is pain. Pain that pulses through her body from shoulder to knee. That beats at her body as the waves beat the shore. But pain is to be borne. This is nothing to the pain of birthing. Pain says one thing only.

Alive.

Still, she must heal.

She scans the rocky tide line and sees it right away. The exact shape and color. Yellow-green, long flat blades torn from forests beneath the sea and now cast ashore. Glistening wet, alive and healthy. She wades into the waves, the cool tide drawing back and forth along her calves. The push, the pull. The glint off the waves. The high reek of the sea, the long smell of death. The shoreline birthing, dying.

She is immune to none of these.

The sea has always been her ally.

On a quiet night at low tide she can hear the world breathing.

She loosens her belt and drops it to her hips, careful not to lose the knife.

She goes to her knees and gently bathes her wounds until the mud is gone and her blood weeps down across her loincloth into the water. Then she stands and walks to shore. She stoops and pulls some of the leaves free of their rocky trap, washes them of sand and crab shell and presses them to her wounds.

They sting. And this too is the sea.

The sea sails through her like a poison now, like a gift. Slowly the pain subsides. She gathers more leaves thick as leather and washes them and presses them to her side, lifts and rebuckles her belt around them to hold them in place.

She walks the shingle beach, eyeing tide pools for food and the cliffs above for shelter. It isn't long before she finds both. A small cache of mussels. *A pair of tiny crabs. And perhaps forty feet above her fifteen yards away a narrow slit in the granite rock face, barely visible, draped in sphagnum moss—the opening to a cave. The crabs she crunches with her teeth and swallows nearly whole. The mussels she palms in her hand two at a time and pummels against the rocks, flicks away the shells with her fingertips and laps the meat inside.*

When she's finished she heads across the beach and climbs a narrow path to the cave.

Some ten feet from the entrance she stops. She scents the air. Pulls the knife from her belt. The knife still bears the dark brown stains of her own blood from the night before—the Cow, in an unexpected bit of treachery from the last of her lost family, has stabbed her just above the hip. And paid for that with his life.

But she has caught the scent of another life.

A familiar one.

Of urine. Of wolf. The cave is marked with wolf-scent. And recent.

She knows the wolf is not normally the enemy. That most will run from her, from any human, rather than confront such an unpredictable opponent. But wolves do not tend to seek a cave unless to whelp and whelping season is over so that with this one care is necessary. She steps softly, stops, listens. Steps closer, the knife poised beside her at shoulder height, her grip firm and ready.

She stops again when she hears the scrabble of paw on rock. The wolf rising. It is less than ten feet away.

Then she hears the growling. Low and raw with intent.

This one is the enemy.

She can picture the wolf clearly. It stands facing her. Its ears are erect. The fur bristles along its massive arched back, its long legs bent for the leap. In its powerful muzzle the lips are curled into a snarl, pulled back away from the six sharp incisors used for cutting and two fangs curved inward for the ripping kill.

It tenses. She can feel it in the dark.

Knows that it can feel her too. Can smell her blood on the knife.

Inside the cave, a sudden rough movement and then the flash of yellow eyes and a hurtling gray-brown body and she leans into its rush, its dive for her throat, leans down and into and off to one side and plunges the knife down and under in a single liquid arc so that the wolf falls crashing back on its spine into the mouth of the cave, thrashing on the blade of the knife thrust up through its neck, paws uselessly tearing through emptiness while she presses her advantage, takes the knife in both her hands and heaves with shoulders, back and forearms, rips upward through muscled neck and bone into the very skull of the wolf, who whimpers once like a small kicked dog and dies.

She inspects her kill.

The wolf is old. White hair along the muzzle, eyes and lower chin. He is male. And large, the height of a deer at the shoulder. His right front paw is mangled. So are his lips, the scarring recent. She opens his mouth. The upper palate is torn too. The wolf has been trapped and somehow he has gnawed his way out of it. She admires his strength and ferocity. But that accounts for his aloneness too and the cave. His wounds, his age.

The wolf is without family.

A blight upon the pack.

She stands away from him, steps forward and peers into the cave. In a few moments her eyes adjust. The cave is not deep, perhaps four times the length of her. Its walls are so narrow in front and back that she can press the palms of her hands to either side—its middle slightly wider. Its walls are high enough for her to stand in comfort though.

No humans have used this cave. No strewn debris or signs of fire. A rare thing. The cave will do.

She takes hold of the wolf's forelegs and drags him inside. At his neck wound she kneels and begins slowly to drink him dry.

In a little over two hours she has created a browse-bed in back of the cave. Fresh soft boughs of pine. In another hour she has collected enough bark, fallen branches, driftwood and stones for a fire. She sparks the fire alight, feeds it bark and twigs and then the more substantial wood crossed in stacks of three.

It is time for the wolf.

She unsheathes the knife. Tomorrow she will need to hone the knife but for now it remains up to the task. She turns the wolf on his back and saws through his neck until the huge head detaches from the body. She hacks off the feet.

Slipping the knife inside his skin, pulling it slightly away from the flesh, she cuts a single line from neck to groin and makes a small circular cut around the anus. She hauls the pelt back off the shoulders—her own shoulders straining—hauls it down over the forelegs, adjusts her position to straddle the wolf and pulls the skin farther over back and chest, haunches and hind legs until finally the pelt is free.

Then another cut down the middle, again from neck to groin, intersecting the cut around the anus, careful shallow cutting now so as not to burst the organs inside. She parts the rib cage and reaches into the body of the wolf with both hands and pulls his insides out in a single mass and lets them spill across the floor.

She separates the liver, heart and kidneys from the rest and sets them aside. These she will roast immediately. On another day in greater hunger or to feed her family she might have cleaned and consumed the other organs as well but there is plenty of meat for now.

She feeds the flames.

She lifts the pelt and drapes it across an outcropping of rock to dry. Her wounds are throbbing.

She sharpens a long greenwood bough and skewers liver, heart and kidneys and holds them low in the fire to sear, turns them once, then lays them across the rocks to cook more slowly.

There is still the wolf's carcass to butcher but that can wait. Her body needs food badly. The wolf's blood is not enough.

She gathers up the organs and throws them down the rock face to the screaming wheeling gulls outside.

* * *

Later, night descending, lying on her browse-bed and listening to the crackling fire and the far-off pounding of the waves she feels an uneasy sense of something she can not quite name. Perhaps it is the cave, the emptiness of it. No sounds but these reach her—the fire and the waves. No restlessness of children. No sleep-sounds from First or Second Stolen. No groaning from the Cow.

It has happened so quickly. Though life can often happen quickly in her world. But two nights ago they were eleven. First and Second Stolen, the Cow, the Girl, the Boy with his clouded eye, the Twins, Rabbit, Eartheater, the baby. All of them together in a much larger cave than this one scattered with their belongings, scavenged for and hunted over many hunts. She is alone now.

Except for the spirit of the wolf she is alone. But the wolf died well. As she herself would die. It is not his spirit that disturbs her.

And she has known aloneness before.

What then?

She hears a descending whistling trill outside. Repeated again and again.

An owl, perched somewhere, calling to his mate.

Stilled by the crash of waves.

so fond of euphem⟨...⟩
turned out to⟨...⟩
ashamed of⟨...⟩
nipples w⟨...⟩
going⟨...⟩
he⟨...⟩

T

"Knock it off, Roger!"

It was the second time he'd sp⟨...⟩
One more time and she'd wade into the ⟨...⟩
shit.

Teenage boys. Good god.

"Aw, hell, Peg. Come on in. It's blazin' hot out there."

He was right of course. It *was* hot. And she'd probably rather be anywhere than at this stupid franks-and-burgers lawn party where she was going to get lemonade instead of beer while her mom and dad, their neighbors and so-called friends guzzled the afternoon away. She felt trapped here. Seemed like she always felt trapped these days. And it was hotter than hell inside the hoodie. But she was not taking it off and she was not going into the damn water.

Certainly not at the urgings of Roger Kaltsas, hanging on the edge of the pool next to her dangling long tanned legs with a boner in his eyes.

"I'm fine, Roger, thank you."

Roger was fourteen to her sixteen, had probably never read a book in his life that wasn't assigned in class—if then—and had not yet learned the words *sotto voce.*

"Bitch," he muttered and kicked off poolside.

"Heard that, asshole," she said. But by then his ears were probably filled with chlorinated water.

It did feel good on her legs though.

At least her mom and dad weren't pressing her to go in anymore. It wasn't that long ago in the scheme of things that she was thirteen and just starting to *fill out* as her mom said—*why the hell were adults*

isms?—and Belle had insisted she do so. That one
be a pretty good row. Belle said she shouldn't be
becoming a lady. Peggy said she wasn't ashamed, but her
ere bigger than her breasts at the moment and she was
wait until they caught up a bit, *is that okay with you?*
er father had sided with her mother at first. But back then,
always came around for Peggy. She could count on it. So that
summer and the summer after, no swimming pool. Then at fifteen
she was completely ready and quite happy to slip into her black low-
cut one-piece spandex.

Now that had changed too.

She wiped a thin line of sweat off her upper lip. Time for that
lemonade, she thought.

She pulled her legs out of the water and hoisted herself up. She
saw that across the yard beyond Mr. and Mrs. Sims working the
hibachi and the grill her mother was walking toward her father, her
father smoking a Winston beneath a birch tree, with two beers in
her hand, one for herself and one for him.

It wasn't fair, dammit.

Lemonade.

"Chris?"

"Yeah, babe."

She handed him the cold Michelob.

"You're a lifesaver, Belle. You know that? Thanks."

She could always anticipate him. He knew it gave her pleasure
to do so.

He took a long pull on the bottle and watched her tilt back her
own. It was her first of the day. She'd have one more with lunch.
Belle was reliable and steady as a clock and two was her absolute
limit. Two beers or two glasses of wine and no hard liquor at all.
While he himself was a scotch man.

On a scorcher like this though, Mich was the ticket.

"Dean wants to talk to you," she said.

He looked past her to the picnic tables. Dean was sitting alone nursing a Budweiser. His bald head in serious danger of sunburn. He was wearing khakis and suspenders over a white T-shirt and his usual hangdog look. And he *was* glancing in his direction. And he *did* look ready to talk.

Christ on a crutch. It was about time.

He smiled at her. "What makes you say that, Belle?"

His tone flustered her, he could see that. But then Belle flustered easy.

"He just . . ."

"Dean wants to talk to me, he'll come over and talk. I'll take a burger when the burgers are ready. Are they ready yet, Belle?"

She took another quick hit on the Michelob. It almost looked involuntary. Like a twitch.

"I don't . . . I'll check."

"Good. And keep an eye on Darlin' over there, will you? She's at that Clapp boy again. She's got to cut that out. Am I right or am I right?"

His daughter was all over the poor kid. Danny Clapp was six years old, with two years and maybe six inches on Darlin'. But he couldn't handle her for a second. She was standing on a picnic bench next to where he was sitting, kissing him all over the face and head and giggling while he tried helplessly to keep her at a distance. *The kissing torture.* He guessed the kid's parents had taught him it wasn't right to push little girls.

Good for them. Not so good for Danny.

Where had he heard or read that? *A kiss was a concealed bite.*

He liked the idea. He guessed his little daughter was a biter.

But Belle was annoyed. Overly so, in his own opinion. Chris thought Darlin'—Darleen really—was just about as cute as cute gets. But Belle had always been a little on the mercurial side when it came to the kids.

"Dammit, Darlin'!" Belle muttered.

He watched her storm across the lawn. For a little woman she had quite a long stride.

He lit another Winston off the first one and pulled on his half-empty beer and that was when Dean chose to get off his butt and approach him.

Chris extended his hand. "Dean."

"Chris."

His grip was surprisingly firm though the palms were smooth and soft.

"Hellova nice day, huh?"

"This time of year, Chris, can't ask for much better."

"You said it. What's on your mind, Dean?"

"That obvious?" He essayed a troubled smile.

"How's Diane?"

"The home's real nice. They're takin' the best care of her I think they can. I want to thank you again, Chris, for putting in the good word for us up there. The lower rate helps. A lot."

"Glad to hear it. Diane's a fine woman. Deserves the best. She improving any?"

"Well . . . she's more comfortable for sure, but . . ."

He didn't want to go *too* far down that path with Dean. Diane wouldn't be improving and they both knew it. Alzheimer's. From what he'd heard, in the advanced stages. He slapped the man lightly on the shoulder. The ash fell off his cigarette onto Dean's white T-shirt sleeve but he didn't seem to notice.

"Hey. Why don't you go in for a swim, old buddy? Clog the drain with all that hair. Do you some good."

Dean tried on another smile. No fit.

"Yeah."

Instead he pulled on his Budweiser.

There was the awkward pause he knew was coming. He leaned back against the birch tree and drank his beer. He saw that across the yard Belle had yanked Darlin' off the picnic bench and was hauling her toward the house.

"You remember telling me to come to you first if I ever thought of selling?"

Here it is, he thought. I knew it.

"Yeah," he said. "But I don't feel like losing my best and only neighbor."

"I just . . . I can't concentrate down at the feed store anymore. Can't find *anyone* who can handle the books the way Diane could. The competition's killing me anyhow. You know I've lost customers I've had for thirty-five years over as little as two cents a pound?"

"They'll come to regret it in the long run. Chain store's not going to extend 'em credit the way you do, prop 'em up for months on end."

Dean seemed not to hear him. He set his bottle down carefully against the tree.

"I'm in a hellova jam, Chris. And I got to be honest. I don't really have the heart to try to pry my way out of it. I spend as much time as I can with Diane up at the home, but I'd like to spend more."

"Understandable."

"So what I want to do is . . . I want to sell it all off and get myself a little one-bedroom up around there so I can be with her these last few months. I don't think she's got much more than that."

He flicked his ash this time before setting his hand down on Dean's shoulder.

"If you're really serious about selling, I'm glad you came to me. Come on down to the office on Monday and we'll see about drawing up some papers. I can't give you the world for the place but I'll give you a fair price."

"I know you will, Chris."

The man seemed looser already.

"Good thing about old friends is, you don't have to worry about getting a lube job," he said.

"That's why I come to you, Chris."

"You were right to. I got an idea. How about you and me getting ourselves a *real* drink? You're a scotch fella like me, am I right?"

"Bourbon."

"I bet we can shake some free."

He picked up Dean's bottle and handed it to him and turned him toward the house.

"You got any buyers for the store yet?"

"Not yet. Couple of feelers."

"Okay, we'll talk about that on Monday too. See what we might be able to do. What the hell, right?"

"Sure. What the hell."

And, arm over his shoulder, he steered Dean across the lawn.

When she got to Darlin' her daughter had Danny Clapp's face in both her hands and was pecking at him repeatedly on the mouth. The boy was in an agony of embarrassment as well he might be, tying to squirm away. Belle was furious.

"I told you! No more kissing! It's . . . just inappropriate. Not to mention a good way to get yourself sick. I catch you at that again I'm gonna take you into the bathroom, you hear me?"

"'Course I hear you, mama, you're yelling in my ear!"

"You watch your mouth, little lady."

This kissing thing. She hated it. There was something unnatural about it, she thought, something perverse.

It had started up only last year. And it wasn't just Danny Clapp or other kids who were the target. Belle herself was, at first. She'd put a stop to that pretty quickly once she realized this was going to become some sort of *thing* with Darlin' and not some occasional show of endearment. She was not one of those mothers who avoided corporal punishment. That was just liberal foolishness—a spanking now and then could be just what the doctor ordered—though she trusted she dealt them out fairly and without any loss of control on her part.

But then this kissing behavior had shifted to Peggy. Even to Brian. Who brooked it exactly once and then, the second time, slapped her. More punishment. That time, for both of them.

Where the hell was Brian, anyway?

"Where's your brother, Darlin'?"

"I dunno. Where we going?"

"Into the house. You're going to sit down and watch some TV. I think you've had quite enough of playing with the other kids for today. You have to learn some control, Darleen Cleek, if you're going to be part of this family. Control, you hear me? You can get yourself a ginger ale if you want one. I'll call you when we're ready to leave."

"Aw, mama . . ."

She marched her into the living room, found the remote and turned on the Sims' TV. Sally Sims was not going to mind. She sat Darlin' in a chair in front of it and handed her the remote. Darlin' took it from her mother with one hand and shoved the thumb of her other into her mouth.

Four years old and she was still sucking her thumb.

She'd always been oral as hell. Nursing her, Belle had been in nearly constant pain. Not like Peggy or Brian. The only worse one was the other one. The one they didn't talk about.

"I don't want to hear a peep out of you until I call you outside, that clear?"

"Yes, mama." She was already flipping channels.

Her daughter was sweet but she had the attention span of a gnat.

Belle sighed and stepped out to rejoin the party.

* * *

Brian Cleek sat in the driveway propped against the Sims' basketball post rolling his Spalding under the palm of his hand and drinking his lemonade and watching the three ten-year-olds devil little Jenny Diva.

Sammy and John were lanky and long-armed like him but Frankie was a fatass. In this case, being a fatass came in handy. They had her against the hedges and she didn't have much wiggle room.

"C'mon," Sammy said, "don't be such a chickenshit."

He pushed her back into the hedges just a little. Just enough to make her aware she was more or less trapped there.

"Stop it!" she said.

"Show it!" fatass Frankie said.

"Show *what?*"

Sammy pushed her a little harder. This time the bushes scratched her bare upper arms.

"Ow! Stop that!"

"Frankie's right. Show it. C'mon."

"What are you *talking* about?"

She really didn't understand. Well, at ten, guys were way ahead of girls. For that matter at Brian's age, thirteen, they still were. The common wisdom—at least as pronounced by his sister Peggy—was that at some point they caught up big-time. But Brian had seen no evidence of that.

He finished his lemonade and set it down, got up and moved back over the macadam and dribbled awhile, watching them.

"Your bush, stupid," John said. "Show us your *bush.*"

"My what?"

He wondered if you even had a bush at ten. He didn't think so. He shot a free throw. Scored. Rebounded the ball.

"Grab her, Frankie," said Sammy.

Fatass did as he was told, grabbed hold of both her arms and turned her toward Sammy. She let out a little mouse-shriek. *Eeeek.* Whether it was Frankie's gripping her too hard or being pressed against his sweaty belly was anybody's guess.

Sammy poked her in her skinny chest, punctuating his words, grinning.

"We. Want. To. See. Your. *Bush!*"

"No!" she said.

Jenny still didn't seem to know what this was all about but she'd started to cry, tears welling up quietly. And then she did know because Frankie reached down to the waistband of her frilly two-piece bathing suit and started to tug it down, the boys all laughing at her as she squirmed every which way and kicked and struggled.

"Hey! Cut that out!"

Mr. French had a half-eaten hot dog in his hand and he was still chewing.

Mr. French was ex-infantry. He didn't just approach. He *loomed.*

"What in the hell do you think you boys are doing here?"

The boys had no answer for that. They looked at one another. Saw no answer there either. How much the man had actually observed coming around the side of the house they didn't know but they were going to catch hell anyhow for messing with a girl and they knew it. Frankie let go of her arm and she stumbled to the tarmac, crying. Sammy, John and Frankie took off like they were rounding third base for home with the ball in play. Even Frankie had a fire under him.

Brian shot another free throw. Sunk it. Rebounded.

Mr. French helped Jenny up. Then turned to Brian, scowling.

"Why were you letting them do that, Brian?"

"Sir?"

The eyes narrowed. The scowl now read contempt.

"Sir? Did you just call me *sir?*"

"Yes, sir."

"Listen, you little smart-ass . . ."

"I was just shooting some free throws, sir."

"Right. Sure you were. And you know damn well you should have stopped them. They're how much younger than you? Three years? Four years?"

"I really wasn't paying attention, sir. I was concentrating on my free throw."

"You . . . jesus christ."

He shook his head in disgust. Brian couldn't have cared less if he was disgusted. He was an ex-marine with a gut on him. Fuck him.

He shot. Hit the rim and missed. Two for three. Not bad but he could do better.

Mr. French led Jenny back to the picnic.

Brian rebounded.

Chris glanced in the rearview mirror at Darlin' sleeping in the back. There was mustard on his daughter's chin. He smiled. Brian got in beside her and slammed the door. She didn't even flinch. *The sleep of the innocent.*

"How'd you do, buddy?"

"Eight for ten, dad."

"Consistently?"

"Just the last time and once before that. I think I'm getting the hang of it though."

"Can't win games unless you hit your free throws."

"I know."

He watched as Belle and Peg approached the back of the Escalade—Belle carrying two beach chairs and Peg a neat stack of wet towels. He hit the auto lock to unlock the tailgate.

"There's Roger," Brian said. "He's got this *major* thing for Peggy."

Cleek checked the rearview again and saw this towheaded pigeon-chested kid walk by with his parents to their own car and it looked like his son was right. The kid was fairly beaming at her. He said something to her that Chris couldn't hear and she shrugged and said something back. Whatever it was turned his smile into a frown.

Busted, he thought. Poor guy.

He couldn't blame the kid for trying though. His daughter had turned into quite a looker.

Belle closed the tailgate and they came around to the passenger side and got in, Peg in back next to her sister and Belle in front and quietly shut their doors.

He turned to his daughter.

"Never went in, huh?"

"Chlorine makes my hair gross."

He laughed. He thought the laugh came out just fine. It usually did.

"Well," he said, "we wouldn't want *that* now, would we?"

He put the Escalade in gear and pulled away.

It was the unpaved road that woke her up. The unpaved road meant they were almost home.

She'd been dreaming about the castle again.

She and Max and Cindy and Teddy—Max was her elephant and Cindy was her rag doll and Teddy was . . . well, Teddy—were out on the lake in her little boat and Teddy was rowing as usual because bears are strong and the breeze was in her hair and it was a nice sunny day. The waves were gentle.

She had her picnic basket with the little-man cookies and bright red candy apples at her feet and she'd already told Cindy that no, they'd have to wait for the candy apples to get warmer so they could get kinda sticky and drippy and easier to eat. She was about to open the basket to give her a cookie instead when the sky went dark and the wind got much stronger and poor Teddy had to struggle. And then it got so dark she couldn't see any of them at all. Like she was alone.

But she wasn't alone. She saw that when the boat landed and the sky cleared a bit and they were all of a sudden right there with her standing in front of the castle. The castle was big and tall and old and crooked-looking and Cindy was scared but Darlin' wasn't.

We'll have our picnic in there she said and the next thing she knew they were in this great big dining room which was crooked too but it had a long wide table so she set the basket on the table and they all sat down while she unpacked the little-man cookies and the red candy apples which were still not sticky enough so she put them back and handed them each a cookie.

"You bite the heads off first, little girl!" came the voice. Which was the witch-who-turned-into-a-wizard-and-then-a-witch-again's voice.

And they turned and saw her there all in black standing by a great big fireplace that hadn't been there at all before and she was waving her crooked black wand at them and she had all those teeth that seemed to turn out from her mouth like dirty nasty forks, curved-like, but even as they screamed at the sight of her she turned into this giant, this flat-headed man with a pointed hat and bulging red eyes and the wand became a club like a table leg and the teeth turned inward like a dog's.

He roared at them and they ran. They ran out the door and the boat was so far away. And she heard her turn back into a witch again and say, real close behind her, scary close, laughing that scary laugh, *I've still got the wand, little girl! I've got the wand!*

And she woke. Still scared like she always was.

And there was the house. Her house. Home.

THREE

The Woman sleeps by the banked embers of the fire, the wolf pelt and browse-bed beneath her.

Her sleep is troubled.

At first this is not so. At first she is running though a thicket, almost dancing through the thicket, graceful and keen with the hunt, eyes wide, all senses alert, her prey in sight. The others are all with her save for the Cow, Second Stolen only steps behind with spear at the ready. The Woman feels a flush of pride in her. Second Stolen has the makings of a leader.

Suddenly a baby wails and she is back in the cave, mating with First Stolen. And if this is not entirely pleasurable, his grunts and thrusts behind her and the smell of his sweat are at least familiar. It is the baby's wail that is unfamiliar. This is not her baby. Nor Second Stolen's. She knows their voices.

"Babai," she says.

She looks around the cave in the flickering light for the source of the sound. Past the pile of axes, hammers, hatchets and other tools and weapons. Past the fire. Past the heap of clothes. And finally there it is. Hanging between three skins, rabbit, fox and human, on the far right wall of the cave. A baby in a knotted clear bag lying in its own piss and shit. The baby writhing, howling. But dead.

Inside this new cave, alone, the Woman turns in her sleep and moans. Her hand goes to the weed-dressed wound in her side. She makes a fist and digs in.

The Woman in her dream uncouples from First Stolen, pushes him back away despite his protests, despite his erection. She gets to her feet and goes to the baby. Stares up at the baby in wonder. How can it be alive and yet dead? She can see its tiny face pressed against the bag.

It snarls at her.

Suddenly the cave erupts in gunfire. First Stolen spins away. Somewhere a woman screams. Another woman presses the face of one of the Twins into the fire and he screeches as his face is burned away and she can hear the sizzle of him amid flying crackling sparks and flames. Then more gunfire, more screaming, groans and the rattle of chains.

Inside this new cave, alone, the Woman's fingers knead her wounds until they bleed.

In her dream it is quiet again. She is surrounded by the dead.

Even the baby now is silent in its bag. She takes it down and lays it on a blanket by the dying embers of the fire and peels the bag away. The baby's eyes are wide so she closes them. She wraps it in the blanket against the morning chill and places a single gray gull's feather on its breast.

In her new cave her hand goes slack at her side. She sleeps.

Four

An hour and a half before dawn Cleek sat showered and shaved and fully dressed at the kitchen table, working on the rifle. He oiled it carefully—and sparingly. Too much oil and a Canadian whitetail could smell you coming a mile away. The rifle was a total honey, a Remington 700, bolt-action, with an ergonomically contoured classic walnut stock and textured grip, a raised cheek piece for rapid scope-to-eye alignment, fitted with a three-by-nine Leupold scope. It took a seven-millimeter Remington Magnum cartridge. He could blast a woodchuck all to hell at three hundred yards with one of those babies. And had.

At three grand it was a bargain.

Belle was at the coffeemaker, pouring. She brought them each a second cup. Black for him. For her, cream and sugar. She sat down and sighed.

"You hear Peg last night?" she said.

"Yep."

"Sick as a dog, Chris."

"I know. Speaking of dogs. You feed them?"

"It's Brian's turn. The dogs can wait."

He put down the brush and sipped his coffee. A good Jamaican blend they sold down at Kristy's, thirty dollars a pound, ground for paper. He lit a Winston and sat back in his chair.

"Peg'll be fine," he said. "Don't worry."

She looked at him with that look she had. She'd gotten that look directly from her mother. There's a saying, *you want to know the kind of woman you're marrying? Check out the mother.* Over the years he'd found that to be more true than not. Her mother had this expression she wore that was half worry and half concentration. Like she had some math problem in front of her and wasn't so sure of her equations.

They sipped their coffee in silence.

He finished his cigarette and drained his coffee and packed away the cleaning gear in his Otis kit—rods, brushes, flannel patches, each in its place. Zippered up, it was about the size of his hand. But then he had big hands. He slipped the Remington into its nylon camouflage floating case and zippered that too.

"I'm gone," he said. He stood up from the table, shouldered the rifle and clipped the kit to his belt. "Wish me luck, hon."

"Luck," she said. "You want a thermos?"

"Nah. I'm floating already."

And then he was out the door. He closed it quietly behind him so as not to wake the dogs out in the barn in front and crossed the yard to the Escalade parked beside Belle's little blue Toyota. It was still a bit chilly in the damp night air but the day promised to be a warm one. The sky was clear and full of stars. He caught the paper-and-wood-smoke smell off the burn barrel. He didn't want it on him.

He slipped into the Escalade and slammed the door.

Let the dogs go crazy now. He wasn't there and it was almost dawn.

Four hours later he was sitting on a rock on a hillside overlooking the wild blueberry patch where last autumn he'd bagged a six-point whitetail buck. He was upwind, surrounded by scrub and pine. It had been a long climb and then a long wait. And so far, nothing. He'd gone through half a pack of Winstons. Two strips of beef jerky and a packet of salted peanuts. He'd resisted the Cutty in his canteen and stuck with bottled water. But maybe it was time to move on.

He took one last scan through the Leupold. All he saw were a pair of black-backed gulls headed for the shoreline about a mile away.

He was down to bird-watching here.

Maybe the stream, he thought. The sun was getting high. A deer might want a drink.

He planted himself in a thicket, behind him a tall stand of white birch. From here he had a clear view of the stream running fast below. He was upwind again and risked a few pulls on the Cutty. Which burned down nicely. With the scope he scanned the stream. He took another pull and then his eye went back to the scope and he damn near fell over on his ass.

The lady was naked to the waist.

She has waded deep into the cool stream. The water is up to her calves and then her thighs. She bends down and cups it in her hands and drinks. The water tastes of stones and fallen leaves.

She peels the brown weeds carefully from her side. They are stained with her blood. They drift on down the stream. She cups more water in her hands and bathes her wounds. This is good. This is soothing. There is only a little blood, a seep of bright red. She splashes water over her face, her arms, her breasts. Kneels and lets the water bathe the wounds in its own way.

She puts her arms out in front of her and feels the slimed stone bottom of the stream and dips her head under. The rocks are smooth as flesh. She is trembling in the water. The water rolls over her and through her like a cold and gentle hand. She lifts her head and gasps for breath and kneels again and that is when she sees it, slowly gliding by.

The stream's gift to her.

It was so swift that had Cleek blinked he'd have missed it.

But he didn't blink.

One moment she was kneeling in water up to her waist, hair dripping over her face and neck and shoulders like some risen—if grimy—nymph in a storybook and the next moment her hand rose up out of the stream and in that hand was a knife, a big one, which plunged back into the water with a speed that astounded him, a sideways slash across her body down and under.

A quick flick of the wrist and the knife surfaced again. And skewered neatly just below the gills was one of the biggest Canadian brook trout he'd ever seen.

Twenty inches easy, a two- to three-pounder.

Another flick of the wrist—harder this time—and she'd thrown the trout clear off the knife to leave it wriggling its death-dance on the shore.

He watched her lay back in the stream, eyes closed, only her breasts and face showing above the water. If her face was not, her breasts were beautiful and lolled gently to either side, the nipples puckered dark and wide.

He held the Remington steady.

A while later she rolled to her knees and stood and waded through the water to the shore. The trout lay still. She stooped, impaled it with the knife again, took two more steps and then stopped.

She appeared to scent the air.

Cleek's hands trembled as he slowly lowered the rifle against the potential glint of sunlight on the scope.

She looked left and right. Far and near. Her gaze passed him over.

He realized he'd been holding his breath ever since she stopped. His heart pounded. He wondered if he was afraid of her.

It was possible.

In her way she was magnificent. Like some large dangerous animal. The wide powerful shoulders, the long ropy muscles of her arms and thighs. She glistened in the sunlight. At this distance without the scope he couldn't see the dirt still matted in her hair though he knew it was there. He couldn't see the scars.

All he could see was this *creature* standing there.

After a time she seemed satisfied she was alone and turned away from him then and stepped out on the path that led around the stream.

Cleek knew what he had to do. There was only one thing he *could* do.

He waited awhile. Then made his way down through the scrub and pitch pine and followed.

She led him along on narrow deer paths, some of which even he didn't know were there though he'd hunted this stretch of land for years. He kept his distance and would have lost her several times were it not for the scope. He was lucky. He was upwind of her all the time. The wind was blowing from the sea and that was where they seemed to be headed.

On a hill overlooking the shore he hunkered down in the tall yellow sweetgrass and watched her pull fresh seaweed from the tide pools and dress her wounds again. The woman was no fool. Seaweed was rich in iron, potassium and iodine and would go a long way fast toward her healing. The wounds were fresh. He wondered how she'd gotten them.

When she'd fastened the weeds to her side with her belt again she paused and stared out to sea. The sea was calm today. Turns and gulls wheeled through the sky beneath long thin streaks of cirrus clouds. The woman seemed to relish the same easy breeze that stirred the grass around him.

He pulled on the scotch and waited.

In a while she turned and walked up the pebbled shoreline to a narrow strip of sand. This, he thought, might be trouble. The sand extended for at least half a mile before falling back to pebble again and there was very little cover. If he needed to follow farther he'd be doing it mostly in the open. But he was lucky. She walked only a few yards and then started up toward the rock face. He scanned it through the slope and saw her destination.

A cave. The woman was headed for a goddamn cave.

He wondered if there were more like her inside.

What the hell, he thought, let's wait and see.

He made himself comfortable. Took a strip of jerky from his pack. Washed it down with some Cutty. When the jerky was gone he lit a Winston and then another and another.

More Cutty. More jerky.

He was not by nature a very patient man unless he was hunting. But he *was* hunting here in a way, wasn't he? And he had plenty of jerky and plenty of cigarettes and could make do with what was left of the whiskey.

He judged it was going be a while.

It was.

Dusk was falling when through the lens of the Leupold he saw the wisps of smoke from inside the cave wave and wrap around the drifting strips of moss. Saw the faint flickering glow from within.

In all that time she had not emerged again.

Another man might have been disappointed. Chris wasn't. Not at all. A little chilly but not disappointed.

That no one else had appeared was a good thing.

Plus he'd given it some thought and had taken the cave's measure.

Steep rough granite surrounded the narrow entrance. A small grassy cliff maybe ten feet directly above. There were other deep indentations in the stone on either side all along the shoreline—worn away by the centuries-old pull and push of wind—but only the single cave as far as he could see.

His guess was that she was tucked in cozy for the night.

He policed his butts and shouldered the Remington. Time to head on home.

It was almost dinnertime.

FIVE

The house was northern white cedar, rot-resistant and durable. It was prefab but certainly didn't look it. The foundation was fieldstone. The stairs and porch were solid granite. Cleek was proud of his house. He'd built it with the money his old man had left him shortly after he and Belle were married and he'd picked up his father's law practice. Two floors, three baths, three bedrooms. They hadn't expected Darlin' but that was okay, Peg didn't mind bunking with her little sister at all. Peg was a good girl.

He pulled up in front of it and the dogs were barking in the barn behind him as soon as he got out of the car. Brian was shooting hoops in the driveway beneath the flood lights. He missed one. Rebounded. Dribbled.

"How's the average?"

He shrugged. "Seven for ten. Pretty consistent."

He wondered if the boy was fibbing to him. Decided it didn't matter much one way or the other. Chris wasn't about to make his son prove it to him.

"Good. That's good."

"You get anything?"

"Do I look like I got anything?"

"Mom's baking us a ham."

"I've got something I need you all to do for me before dinner."

"Okay."

"Wait out here."

"Sure, dad."

***

"I should turn down the ham," Belle said.

"Fine, you do that."

She turned the oven down from two fifty to two hundred. The ham was bone-in, glazed with a brown sugar, mustard, lime and ginger sauce. It needed to be basted every twenty minutes. She didn't want it to burn.

"Come on," he said. "Come with me."

"Me too?" said Darlin'.

He smiled and took her by the hand. "Sure, sweetie. You too."

He led them down the front steps across the stone and gravel path to the fruit cellar just left of the barn. Peg plodded along behind her. He waved to Brian.

"Follow us, son."

What the hell's he want down there this time of the evening? Belle thought. *I'm cooking his dinner.* There wasn't any point in asking though.

It was a wooden cellar door painted barn red, chipped and rough in places, set at a slight angle off the ground. Belle was still lobbying him for a steel one. It would help keep the weather out of her preserves. But she guessed that for Chris a new cellar door just wasn't a priority. Or maybe the old one reminded him of his father's—back when they still had the farm. She didn't know.

He used the key on the padlock. Hauled the door up and open.

"Watch your step now."

At the base of the narrow stone stairway he turned on the light. A single bright bulb overhead.

Belle had never much liked the cellar. It smelled of old dead air, musty, of earth and mold and rust. She could hear crickets somewhere nearby chirping away. There was shelving on all sides. Her preserves were neatly arranged on a pair of them directly to her left. The preserves were her only reason to go down here. Below them just above the old concrete sink, were jars of nails, screws and brackets that Chris hardly, if ever, used. All of them opaque with grime. His father's old tools. On the floor, a trunk, a pile of board games the kids had grown out of, a tricycle with a broken wheel which had once belonged to Brian—Chris had planned to fix that up for Darlin' but bought her a new one instead—an old rusty wagon and a Flexible Flyer which hadn't been flexible for years.

Piles of junk. Empty water and Clorox bottles. Aluminum cans. Paint cans. Boxes of her mother's seventy-eight-rpm records, probably all warped by now. Belle's old ironing board and iron. Boxes of magazines and books. *Why were they saving textbooks that belonged to Peggy ten years ago?* A folding table-and-chairs set that would probably never see a card party again. Standing lamps. Table lamps. A Polaroid camera.

Chris couldn't let go of anything.

Which is why what he said surprised the hell out of her.

"I'm gonna need you to clean out all this junk from the south end of the cellar. To about midway through. Sweep the floor."

Peggy sighed. "*Before* dinner?"

"Yes, honey. Before dinner."

"Why?"

"Because your dad wants you to. You don't have a problem with that now, do you, Brian?"

"Nah. Where do you want us to put all this stuff?"

"Throw it in the dump trailer. If it's small and burnable, put it in the burn barrel. You'll need some gloves. There's a few pair out in the barn. You feed the dogs yet?"

"It's Peggy's turn."

"Peg?"

She sighed again. The girl was big on sighing these days.

"Oh, all right. I'll feed the dogs. I'll get the gloves."

"Good girl."

Belle watched her trudge up the stairs.

"Are there mice down here?" asked Darlin'.

"Could be," Chris said.

"Should I get some cheese?"

Chris patted her head. Even Belle had to smile. Their daughter was pretty adorable.

"Nah, honey," Chris said. "I don't think that's a good idea."

He turned to Belle. "You organize things down here, okay? With the three of you? Shouldn't take too long. Keep this little one out of trouble. I've got things to do upstairs."

"Chris? Why are we doing this? I mean . . ."

"You'll see. Trust me on this one."

She repressed her own urge to sigh. *Trust me* was one of his favorite phrases. Usually she did—and things worked out okay in the end. But there was something really odd about this. *Why now?* She guessed he was off on one of his little projects again. When that was the case there was no stopping him. She'd known Chris Cleek for over twenty years and was fully aware that for a lawyer her husband could be a highly impulsive man. Only last summer he got it into his head at ten in the evening to paint the barn doors a darker shade of red than the rest of it. Thought it would look better. So there he was, working under the floodlights until well after twelve, coming to bed smelling of Dutch Boy and turpentine.

She called to him on the stairs.

"Check the oven, will you? Maybe do a basting for me?"

"Will do, cap'n," he said.

Agnes, George and Lily greeted Peg warmly. To say the least. They were all over her when she stepped into the cage—the entire north side of the barn—to retrieve their food and water dishes, presenting heads and necks and floppy ears for scratching and three warm wet tongues. They were big dogs. Forty to fifty pounds at least she guessed. You had to watch your balance when they got up on their hind legs on you. She indulged them awhile. In truth that while she griped at having to do the chore she didn't really mind. How could you hate handling a dog?

Even Agnes, the mother, who could be nippy—*who could be* damn *nippy with everybody but Peg, even with her own pups*—elicited a kind of warmth in her exceeded only by her affection for Darlin'. Peg didn't question it. It was just there.

Dogs were like big sloppy children.

Unless of course you fucked with them.

When she stepped outside the cage to hose off the dishes and closed the chain-link door they all set to barking. She thought that nothing else on earth has a voice like a coonhound. It was a voice bred to command the night. To be heard from literally miles away, trailable in full darkness. In the enclosed space of the barn they were like a series of small sonic booms.

They quieted again when she returned with the dishes, snuffing at her legs and heels as she set them in their given places along the concrete floor. Then shrunk away when she brought in the hose. The dogs were wary of the hose. The hose meant fresh water or a clean floor but it could also mean a bath, which they didn't particularly want. Or under higher pressure, in the hands of Brian or her father, occasionally worse.

She didn't like to think about that.

She filled the three water dishes and the one inside the doghouse, rolled the hose up and draped it on its hook, pried open the lid of the metal food bin and set to scooping out kibble. The dogs dug in. She filled the dish inside the silent doghouse too—filled that one carefully and gingerly.

She shut the cage door and found three sets of work gloves neatly stacked on a shelf amid her father's tools.

She left the dogs amid chomping sounds and flying drool.

They were always hungry.

As always she felt a twinge of guilt at closing the barn doors on them. Cutting them off. There was a time they were allowed free run of the yard. Now they only got out on nights when her father and his friends wanted to do some coon hunting. Which wasn't all that often anymore. And these guys were meant to run.

They were hunters. Her dad said they could pull down a deer if he let them.

As always she put those thoughts behind her.

She had other chores to do. She had not the slightest idea why.

First things first, Chris thought. He dialed Betty's number from the kitchen. Betty was his paralegal, his office manager, his secretary. And she never minded him calling on a Sunday.

She had caller ID and picked up on the second ring.

"Hi, Betty," he said. "Just want to run a few things by you, okay?"

It was okay. It was always okay.

Betty was a treasure.

"I won't be in until after lunchtime tomorrow. If at all," he said.

Anything wrong? she said. Real concern in her voice, bless her. *No, there was nothing wrong, nothing at all.*

"Just some business I need to take care of here. We've got the Oldenberg will and power of attorney ready for her signature, right? And she's due in at ten. Good. We're also expecting the police report on that Blakely business. That kid's gonna be the death of his poor parents. One more thing. Give Dean Bluejacket a call. He's supposed to come in tomorrow morning to talk to me about his property. Tell him I'm tied up here and I'll meet him for lunch on Tuesday, say noon. Then if the phones are quiet you can put the machine on and take off early. How's that sound?"

It sounded good.

"'Night, Betty. You have a good one."

He heard a shrill scream from outside and the screen door flew open and suddenly Darlin' was hugging his leg for dear life. And there was Brian behind her holding a small, very dead brown mouse by the tip of its tail. He dangled it into her sight lines, grinning. She squealed and giggled and buried her face in his pants leg.

But then she couldn't resist. She peeked up at her brother.

He opened his mouth and pretended he was going to eat it.

"Eeeeewwww!" she said.

Chris smiled at his son and shook his head. *Kids.*

"Burn barrel," he said.

And remembered he was supposed to baste that damn ham.

Chris was late for dinner. Baked ham, corn on the cob, baked green beans and mashed potatoes. Everybody seated around the table except him. Brian was mowing the food down. He'd want seconds. Peggy was barely picking at it. Darlin' was swirling it around into a big goopy mess with her fork. It was Belle's turn to sigh.

What the hell was Chris doing out there?

He was acting very strange.

He'd taken down the five-by-nine-inch authentic wide-mesh fishing net off the west wall of the living room and denuded it of all its ornamental starfish and shells, folded it and taken it out to the fruit cellar. Then she'd heard him on the stairs just now and looked out from the kitchen to see him carrying four of Brian's plastic-coated hand weights, which the boy never used—the weights were a total waste of money—across the foyer and out the door. She crossed to the dining table and through the window in front of it saw that the weights were going into the fruit cellar as well. By then the food was already on the table.

She opened the window and leaned out.

"Chris!"

"Be just a second, hon!"

She closed the window and sat down to eat with her kids. She buttered and salted her corn. The corn was good this year.

Finally the front screen door slammed and Chris was at the table, smiling at them. He sliced a piece of ham and cut it into pieces. Tasted it. Chewed.

"Good," he said. "Um . . . a little cold." Like he was surprised.

She almost laughed. What did the man expect?

"Want me to zap it for you?"

He handed her the plate.

She didn't know whether it was the hammering or the dogs that woke her.

She rolled over into his empty space and switched on the standing bedside lamp he would read by with its too-expensive pale silk lampshade and filled the room with sixty watts of light. She got out of bed and found her robe and belted it around her waist. The hammering stopped. Then continued.

She padded barefoot down the hall to the stairs. She had nearly fallen down this staircase once when she was six months pregnant with Brian riding delicate in her womb so that now as ever since her hand went automatically to the railing.

At the bottom she walked to the front door and looked out the window panel. The hammering had stopped again.

The door to the fruit cellar was flung wide and she could see his shadow moving below in the flickering light.

"What's he doing?"

She jumped at the voice and then had a single strange moment of utter disorientation. Sitting on the couch in the dark in the palest shaft of moonlight, staring out the window, her bathrobe pulled tight around her, arms crossed beneath her breasts, Peg might have been a younger Belle, the Belle of twenty years ago, a slim young woman sitting alone on that very same couch in just that pose and bathed in just that light of the waning moon, wondering. Wondering had she done the right thing.

Marrying him.

"Damn, Peggy. You scared the hell out of me."

"Sorry. I couldn't sleep."

"Well, try. School in the morning."

"What's dad doing?"

"We'll find out tomorrow. Go to bed, Peg. It's late."

She watched her daughter place one bare foot on the floor and pivot her weight off the couch in a single smooth motion, tighten her belt and move gliding to the stairs. Again she had the uncanny sense that she was seeing herself giving in to the necessities of life in some other distant time.

Belle had been a soft and pretty woman then just like her daughter.

Now she was all angles.

"'Night, mom," she said.

"'Night, Peg."

When she was gone and Belle heard her bedroom door click shut and saw the shaft of light disappear from under her door she peered out the window again and heard the dogs barking and then went to where her daughter had sat upon the couch.

It was still warm.

Six

She awakens before dawn, before the gulls and the terns. She hears only the gentle susurration of the waves. In the dim last moonlight she inspects her wounds. Her eyes need little light. The wounds are puckering, knitting, a wide purple bruise surrounding each and connecting at her side as one.

She stretches on all fours like a cat, tailbone high, working out the soreness the hastily fashioned browse-bed and damp night air have left throughout her body. The fire has fallen to ashes now. Beside them lie the blackened bones of wolf and fish.

She crouches down at the entrance to the cave. She studies the dawn. The graying sky. The first gull cry.

It is time to depart this place. She is still not far enough away from where she left her family and the others cold and dead. She has cut a wide pouched sling from the pelt and in it she now places the wolf's left rear thigh. All that is left of him. She drapes it over her shoulder. Across the other shoulder, the remainder of the pelt. It will be colder to the north.

She belts the knife and steps outside.

Cleek has drenched the net in water overnight and attached Brian's weights to the corners at either end. The net doesn't so much drop over her as it *plummets* over her. The woman has fallen to her knees instinctively, twisting furiously inside it. Raging, howling.

He's got to be fast.

He half jumps, half slides down the path from the grassy roof of the cave to the entrance, the Remington over his shoulder. The woman has her knife free and she's standing, slashing. Had she not gotten so tangled up at first she'd be out by now. Free. And that's a goddamn chilling thought.

She's roaring something.

"Deamhan! Sainmahiniu liom fuil! Deamhan!"

Whatever the fuck *that* is.

The pelt has twisted in the net in front of her. To slash through to him it seems she must slash through the pelt. The man stands in front of her and she can smell his fear and can smell his excitement. The man wants to go to her. The man does not.

"Devil! I'll drink your blood! Devil!"

Her arm rises, falls. Her arm speaks her desire.

Kill.

The man dares a single step closer. Her own legs are entangled in his web. She cannot free them without doing herself serious harm. She slashes forward instead through the pelt and through the net and feels her arm finally come free of him, this extension of him, this man-thing. She lurches forward.

Falls.

He sees murder in her eyes. Or worse.

"Deamhan!"

Cleek stands over her. Not too close. She's still got that pig-sticker of a goddamn knife well in hand. And god, he thinks, look at those teeth! But she's tangled up pretty good now. Only that one arm free. That's free enough.

"I'm afraid I can't understand a fucking thing you're saying, lady."

The butt end of the Remington makes a satisfying *thunk* against her thrashing head. So that then she stops thrashing altogether.

Cleek allows himself to breathe.

***

The really hard, nervous part is untangling her. He has no choice but to do it right then and there in front of the cave because there's no way in hell he's going to drag a sodden net with eighty pounds of weights attached—not to mention the woman herself—all the way back to the Escalade. He uses her own knife. He tests it with his thumb and it's far sharper than his own. Carbon steel honed to a feather edge with a bolted wooden handle. His best guess was that it would date back to the 1930s or '40s. A real antique.

They made these things better then.

But he has to use both hands to cut her free, particularly her legs and that means putting the Remington aside and though he'd hit her pretty hard he doesn't like to think what she'll be wanting to do to him when she wakes. Even unconscious she looks formidable. Easily as tall as he was, maybe taller. Scarred, heavily calloused hands with long thin fingers. Powerful back, thigh and shoulder muscles. Cleek thinks of Olympic swimmers. Washboard stomach. In fact it looks to Cleek like her large-nippled breasts are the only fat on her body anywhere.

There are scars all over her.

Where the hell has she come from? he thinks.

And where the hell has she been?

As he pulls her free of the net he sees that he's neglected to remove a single small brown ornamental starfish from within its folds. He's overlooked it. He shakes his head.

With her it will be wise to overlook nothing.

He digs the plastic cable ties out of his pack and binds her feet together and binds her hands behind her back. Her skin is surprisingly warm and pleasing to the touch. As though she burns at some slightly higher temperature than he does.

He unpacks and spreads out the beach towel that said TIME FLIES WHEN YOU'RE HAVING RUM and rolls her onto it and starts dragging.

Twenty minutes later with several stops for his Evian bottle he has her up and into the back of the Escalade. It's only then that she stirs.

He uses the Remington on her forehead before she comes fully awake.

She'd have one hell of a headache. But he doesn't want her awake for quite some time yet. Though the prospect of that time thrills the hell out of him.

He puts the car in gear and heads home. The Escalade purrs.

In his mind, so does Cleek.

SEVEN

Monday morning and nobody home, just as he knows it will be. The kids at school. Belle and the ladies of the Rotary Youth Exchange at their weekly tea-and-coffee klatch over at Trudy Forget's place. He has the house to himself. And the cellar.

Like his father before him Chris has always been a handy kind of guy. He can cane a chair, replace the drive belt on a lawn mower, paper a wall or fix your plumbing like a pro. So outfitting the fruit cellar has hardly been a challenge at all.

The only question in his mind is, will she stay out or will he have to whack her one again.

He hauls her up over his shoulder in a fireman's carry and then eases her carefully down to the lawn while he opens the cellar door. Hauls her up again and walks her down the stairs. *Damn! This lady stinks!* First thing he is going to have to do is wash her down. With extreme prejudice. And he is going to need a shower himself just as soon as this is over.

The entire south side of the cellar is clean save some empty one-by-twelve pine shelving starting midway up from floor to ceiling. He sits her propped against the wall. Stands back a moment. Catches his breath. Watches her.

She doesn't move. *Good.*

He takes two cable clamps from the shelf behind him—self-locking, polymer and stainless steel—kneels down and slips her wrists into them. From these depend a pair of high-tension tow cables threaded through sturdy eye bolts in the wall above her head. These he's fastened to a single cable which connects to a hand-cranked winch bolted to the wall beside him.

Cleek walks over to the winch and ratchets her up.

When she's upright in a standing position he adjusts her legs so that they conform to the pair of clamps bolted to the wall behind her, slips her ankles inside and tightens the nuts with his crescent wrench.

He smiles.

She hangs there like a rag doll.

His rag doll.

Now that he can safely risk it he decides she demands closer inspection.

He checks her hands. Calloused beyond belief. Nails thick and cracked and yellowed. They'll need some trimming. Her toenails too.

He runs his hand over the matted poultice at her side. Get rid of that. Fix it up with bacitracin and a proper bandage, first thing.

Then her collarbone, her breastbone, covered with scars old and new, large and small. He traces the smooth wide white scar from breast to hip. The scar above her eye that runs through the blasted eyebrow to her ear.

The scars are a roadmap of rough living.

She's been through lord knows what.

What he has here is a survivor. That means she is going to be . . . very interesting.

The Woman slinks awake.

Perhaps it is his hands upon her that have awakened her, she doesn't know. But she is very aware of them now. They sweep across her belly, her breast, her neck. They are not hard hands but they're not soft either. She doesn't move a muscle but she does take stock. She is in a cool damp room. Metal encases her wrists and ankles. There is strain in her arms. Her head hurts badly.

The man touches her face, lifts her chin. Drops it. She lets it drop, slack, to her chest. He lifts her chin again and then with the fingers of

his other hand pries open an eyelid. The eye does not so much as twitch.
He is not aware of this but she sees the man quite clearly. His face is
soft. Shaven. His hair is thin and slick to his scalp. His eyes squint
with . . . what? concern? *Does he fear he's hurt her too badly?*

He hasn't.

Cleek is looking for dilation of the pupils. A sign of brain trauma. He
doesn't see it. She's just out, that's all. He continues his inspection.

There's a new purple bruise along her cheekbone. He didn't put
it there. He'd hit her on the forehead.

The woman is fascinating.

Her upper lip is scarred like most of the rest of her. The lower lip
has fallen open.

He wonders about the teeth. Her breath is foul.

He lifts the left side of her upper lip as though checking out
a dog's mouth or a cat's. The teeth range in color from brownish
yellow to a kind of mossy green—they clearly haven't been brushed
in years, if ever—and the wisdom tooth on this side has gone to
black. The canine almost looks to have been filed sharp. Certainly
it's jagged. The gums though are a healthy pink.

On the right side the wisdom tooth is completely missing. And
now he can see definite signs of rough filing, not only on the canine
but on the incisor too. It dawns on him exactly what this indicates,
exactly what he's seeing.

It dawns on him too late.

The woman's head whips suddenly to the right. The jaws snap
down.

The tip of his middle finger! Jesus christ it's missing! It's gone!

The finger gouts blood all across her chin, her neck and breasts.
He waves the hand as though he'd hit himself with a hammer, hit
his thumb hammering in a nail, shakes it to negate this pain which
burns and throbs and runs right up his arm, shakes it to make it go

away. This impossible sudden thing. His blood sprays him too. His face, his shirt.

"Ahhhhh! Fucking *bitch!*" he screams.

He takes a shaky step backward and almost stumbles. Rights himself.

"Bitch!" he screams again. His voice sounds wrong to him. A huge hoarse bellow. The kind of sound his goddamn father might have made.

His eyes lock with hers. A hint of a smile in her eyes. *She's smiling.* The cunt is smiling! He watches her—*hears her* chew. Teeth against bone. His bone. *Once.* Teeth grinding. *Twice. Three times.*

She swallows.

The Woman has tasted him. His flesh is hers. His blood is thick and as sweet on her lips as honey. So that it does not matter what comes after, doesn't matter when he comes at her with his fist flailing, when her lips split and the pain rages through her head again far worse than when she woke. It doesn't matter because she has warned this man and he has taken note and she has taken his measure.

She has tasted him.

Cleek hits her again and again. He's savage. He's every bit his father now. She's bleeding from the mouth and one eye is shot with blood but she won't shut her eyes and that smile won't go away and he realizes he's screaming, spitting like a snake and blood is flying from her mouth, both of them painting the cellar floor a spackled red until finally at the brink of his own exhaustion the damned eyes close and she hangs limp in front of him.

He backs away, dazed by what he's done and what's been done to him.

And what he says next will make no sense at all to him an hour later.

And an hour after that, it will.

"That's just *not civilized behavior!*" he shouts.

It is exactly then that the pain truly washes over him. Not only from his bloody hand clutched tight in the other but, he thinks, from every bone and muscle in his body. His lungs are burning.

He has one more look at her, blood dripping from her mouth to the dusty floor.

You and I will have a little talk about this, he thinks. We're not done yet.

He shambles toward the stairs.

EIGHT

I'm losing them again, she thought. Hell, if I didn't have my looks I'd lose them even more. How can almost an entire classroom go *sullen* on you? How did you make geometry into something bigger and more important than simple chalk figures on a blackboard?

It had been bigger and more important for her when she was their age. As a teenager Genevieve Raton had looked at another blackboard in another town and saw the positions of the stars and planets, crop circles, the pyramids of Egypt, the topology of a mountain range. The straightedge for her held the principle of order. From the compass flowed grace, symmetry, even mystery.

Teaching was probably just not rooted in her blood though, she thought. Descartes was. Physics was. But why should that make all the difference? It hadn't to her. Her own high school teacher was no genius at teaching. It was the *subject* that hooked her, not the man. Mr. Boorman always had yellow sweat stains circling the armpits of his starched white shirt, for god's sake.

At least she had her youth going for her. It was only her second year at this, still pretty much fresh out of college. So the kids could relate to her a bit on a personal level. And the boys could relate to the fact that she was pretty.

They just couldn't relate to geometry.

Apathy abounded.

She sighed and immediately regretted it. You had to be upbeat with kids no matter what.

"Okay, so who can tell me what a scalene triangle is?"

"Three unequal sides!"

That was Jack. Jack again. Her single truly attentive geometry student—who couldn't help but blurt it out. Thus making him immediately the object of major scorn from the rest of the class. *Brownie.*

"That's right. But didn't we forget to raise our hand on that one, Jack?"

"Sorry, Ms. Raton."

But he wasn't. The little guy was grinning. A bit embarrassed by his own enthusiasm, maybe, but not sorry. In a way she had to admire his pluck. The courage of a true nerd, born and raised. It didn't seem to bother him at all that Eric Durdaller was snickering at him one desk behind.

Eric and his buddy Gary Franck seemed interested in one thing only in her class.

Her tits.

"All right. What other kinds or triangles are there? Name them for me."

Silence. Vast and deep. Only Jack's hand in the air. *Come on, you guys, you* know *this!*

There was no way she was going to Jack for an answer. Maybe Peggy Cleek, she thought. Peggy had started off the year as one of her best students. But she'd fallen off considerably since. She still had her good days but now, you never knew.

She walked the aisle. Caught Tommy Barstow staring at her legs.

Peg seemed to be doodling in her notebook.

"Peggy? Taking copious notes, as usual, right?"

She was going for a wry tone here, not a mean one. But she wasn't entirely sure she'd pulled it off. It had been an exasperating day so far. She was having a lot of them. And the look on Peggy's face was almost *pained.* An overreaction, she thought, in any case, even if she did sound a little mean.

"Ummm . . . just some notes, yeah . . ."

"So, what other kinds of triangles are there, Peggy?"

She looked around as though the answer were written on the walls somewhere.

"Scalene?"

And Genevieve guessed that the rest of the class had been paying more attention than Peggy had at least because that drew a pretty good laugh. Peggy flushed. Then clutched her stomach. *Dear god,* she thought, *is this girl going to get sick in my classroom? Over a* triangle?

"Please. May I be . . . ?"

"Yes, Peggy, you may. Sure."

The girl was out of her seat and out the door in a matter of seconds.

And then the whole class fell hushed for a moment. All you could hear was the door slamming rattling the glass window and then the uncomfortable shuffle of feet. What was going on here? She'd guessed menstrual pains at first. Now she wasn't sure. Did the class know something she didn't know?

It was Jack who broke the silence.

"Isosceles. And equilateral. Right?"

"Right, Jack."

As she walked back to the blackboard past his desk she was tempted to pat him on the head like the good little doggie he was. She resisted that temptation.

When the class broke for recess Peggy still hadn't come back from the girls' room. Genevieve went to her desk and opened her folder, flipped a few pages. Notes, doodles, the usual. She stopped at a drawing. It was not a bad rendering. Done in black felt-tip pen. A small house, like a dollhouse—but empty—within a small, equally empty room. Something canted in the angles of each.

She closed it just as Peggy came in, head down, hands shoved into the pockets of her oversize hoodie.

"You okay, sweetie?"

"Yeah. I just need to get my stuff."

She watched the girl gather up her folder and her books and backpack and thought no you're not. You're not okay at all.

You, Peggy Cleek, bear watching.

Brian was tired of shooting these damn hoops. Despite what his father might think he wasn't tall enough or fast enough to be really good at the game no matter how long and lean he'd gotten or how many free throws he landed. Nor would he ever be. His competition on the playground was proof of that if he ever needed any. He drifted over to the tetherball pole. A game in progress.

Cyndi was hitting clockwise and Walter counterclockwise. A bunch of kids were hanging around watching. Walter was easily a foot and a half taller than she was, but Cyndi was a tiger at competition and practically a grasshopper at jumping. *Tiger and grasshopper. Kung-fu tetherball?* At first Walter looked to have the advantage, lazily and confidently using his height to fist-pop one over her head. But it wasn't too long before Cyndi got under the ball and stayed there. And soon she was whipping his ass easily. Outmaneuvering him every time. The girls were giggling. The boys were split—about half of them cheering her on and the other half solemn.

Their macho at stake along with Walter's.

Meanwhile Cyndi kept pounding the ball toward the sky while Walter stumbled around flustered missing most of what she was whacking at him and minutes later it was over. The ball clunked against the pole and wound down.

Cyndi had barely broken a sweat. Walter looked bushed. He slunk away to the water fountain.

This was the same kid who used to call him *chubs* in the second grade, the same kid who gave him a bloody nose in the third. Brian felt no pity.

"Who's next?" she said.

"Me," said Brian.

Why not? It didn't look like any of the other guys were going to risk it.

"Your win, your serve," he said and stepped to his side of the pole.

At first he thought he had her. He returned, she returned, he returned again. She hit a good one over his head but he stepped in and slapped it, fast, and damn near hit her in the face. He wouldn't have exactly wanted to do that but he wouldn't have minded either. But she ducked just in time. And Cyndi was nothing if not agile. She waited for the next go-round and then started slamming it, darting all over the place and pretty soon he was helpless.

Thunk.

"Damn, you're good."

She smiled. "Why thank you, Mr. Cleek."

He smiled back at her. "My father's Mr. Cleek. I'm Brian, remember?"

"Why thank you, *Brian.*"

He turned and threw her a little wave as he walked away. Cyndi liked him. Had for a while. He could practically feel her eyes on his back.

As for him, he was probably as pissed off as Walter was. Maybe more so. But he wasn't about to show it. No way. Let her think he's cool with it. Hey, you lose one every now and then. No problem.

He walked into his empty classroom and at his desk pulled out his backpack and from it, his pack of Trident Wild Blueberry Twist gum. Unwrapped a stick and chewed it awhile until the flavor began to fade. Then he walked over to Cyndi's desk right beside his where she'd left her oversize Hello Kitty purse. He unzipped it and found her hairbrush and worked the gum deep into the bristles, pressing it flat with his thumb. Returned the brush to the purse and zipped it up again.

Cyndi was no Lady Gaga in the put-together department but she'd be sweaty and tangled when she returned from recess and she was vain about her pretty long blonde hair.

He went outside again and watched the basketball game a while until the bell rang. The class filed in. Feet scuffling the floor, the scrape of chairs.

Cyndi flashed him a smile as she sat and sure enough, unzipped her purse and took out her compact and hairbrush.

He got her on the first brisk stroke.

"Owwww!"

The brush wasn't exactly stuck there but to get it out she was going to lose some hair.

"Cyndi?"

"There's like, glue or something in my . . ."

"Hang on a minute."

He got up and walked over, bent in close to her hair and checked it out.

"Gum," he said.

He stood. Looked at Walter seated with his jock buddies way in back.

"Dude," he said. "A girl beats you at tetherball and you . . ."

He shook his head.

Walter just stared up at him, clueless. Half the girls in class crucified the poor guy right then and there.

"Lemme see if I can . . ."

He took the brush in both hands and gently moved it side to side.

"Owww! That hurts!"

"Jeez, Cyndi. I'm sorry."

"It's okay. I'll do it. Thanks for trying."

She looked up at him and he could see that she bought it. That concerned look he had. He could do that look for anybody. His father. His mother. Anybody.

She took a breath and pulled it free.

"Damn! Damndamn*damn!*"

Yeah, a very nice chunk of wispy blonde hair.

NINE

She wakes to the taste of blood in her mouth. Her own now. She licks her lips. They're dry and cracked and sore. Her head is pounding. She stands. It hurts to stand. There is something pressing into the center of her back, pushing her forward. A ledge of polished wood. She adjusts herself as best she can to accommodate it to the long muscles of her back, taking pressure off her spine. Her eyes have adjusted to the meager shaft of light knifing through the bottom of the doorway so that when she looks above her head she can see that in her suspension her hands have turned a dark purple. She works her fingers together and apart and slowly the feeling returns to them so that they pulse with ache.

She takes in her surroundings. Stone walls, glistening damp. A long narrow room with stairs directly opposite her leading up to a wooden door. Out of her reach to her left, wooden ledges like the one pressing into her back. Glass jars upon them—and inside the jars, food. She sees tomatoes, greens, and bright red and yellow jars of what she knows to be sweets. Her mouth begins to water. The taste of blood runs thin now.

Between her feet the man has left a large yellow bowl. She knows what this is. This is to collect her piss and shit.

Across the room she sees an old trunk, a wagon, metal traps for small game, hammers, tools, a saw. Should she find a way to free herself these last items can be of use to her. She hears dogs barking in the distance. It is impossible to know how far away.

She hears metal scrape on wood, metal on metal. The door is flung open. Daylight floods the room, for a moment blinding her. The man stands at the top of the stairs. He pauses. There is something in his hand. In the wash of bright afternoon light she cannot see what it is. Only

that it is small and pointed in her direction. Then her eyes adjust as he
descends the stairs.

Cleek walks to within three feet of her and stops.

"So you like to bite?" he says.

He waves his bandaged finger in front of her eyes.

The woman just stares at him. He remembers that he has never liked a cat's stare. A cat will look you in the eyes just as it's about to spring.

"You can't understand a word I'm saying, can you. I get that. But I can damn sure make you understand who's in charge here."

And then she *does* spring. Maybe a whole six inches before the cable clamps on her wrists stop her dead. He thinks, that's gotta hurt.

He slips the Springfield .45 pistol into the front of his jeans and takes the Peltor hunting earmuffs out of his back pocket. When he puts them on his voice is coming at him from a distance. He likes the sound of it. His voice like in a dream.

"I've got kids to raise around here, lady, and disobedience is not something I want them to witness. They're very good kids and I would very much like to introduce them to you. But if you're not going to be nice, if you're going to be disobedient, well, I can't do that, now can I."

All he gets is that cold stare. Those scary eyes. But he's not afraid of her now. He's seen what she can do and from where he's standing, it ain't much.

"Plus," he says, "I need to feel better about losing my finger."

He takes out the .45 and shows it to her. Puts it right up in her face. Clicks off the safety.

"Ever see one of these?"

She has. Those hard eyes widen for a moment. Her head rolls away to the side.

"Makes a loud sound, right?"

He jumps at her.

"Boom!"

She doesn't react. Just stares again.

"Makes an even louder sound in a tight space. I'll show you. But first I need a backstop. No ricochets."

There's a three-foot length of six-by-six raw lumber leaning against the wall. He puts the gun to her cheek so she won't get any more biting ideas and sets the block on the shelf behind her, standing it up lengthwise so that now there's about eight inches of wood in back of her shoulder just next to her left ear.

He takes two steps back, aims, and as the woman closes her eyes against what she thinks is coming, he shifts his aim left to the wood and fires.

Even with the earmuffs on it's a huge sound in that cellar. Wood splinters and flies. The woman screams. The scream turns into a roar. Her head trembles from the concussion and then rocks from side to side. He pulls off the earmuffs and stuffs them in his pocket.

She's moaning. She opens and closes her mouth over and over like a fish gasping for breath on dry land. Blood seeps over her jaw and trickles down her neck.

He's blown out her eardrum.

And that'll teach you to bite, now won't it, he thinks.

The eyes open. He reads both pain and anger there. But mostly pain.

"I feel better about my finger now," he tells her.

He smiles. Actually the pain is not too bad by now. Seven hundred fifty milligrams of Vicodin has helped a lot.

"I'll be back in a little while. With the wife and kids. And you be nice, or . . ."

He raises the gun, points it at her other ear, meaning to tell her that he can blow out that eardrum too but she misreads him, begins to struggle violently against the clamps and she's howling again, throwing herself back against the shelving and forward against the clamps. All hell is breaking loose down here.

He lowers the weapon.

She quiets immediately.

Good girl, he thinks. *See? You can learn.*

He heads for the stairs but something stops him. The quiet. It seems suddenly unnatural after all that commotion. He glances back over his shoulder. The woman is as still as a statue.

Watching him.

In the dark she tilts her head to let the blood drain out of her ear. The dark is roaring at her like storm waves against the shore and she thinks of those waves and that shore and wonders how far away they are from where she stands now and if she will ever see them again or if she will simply die trying.

It will be one or the other.

And soon.

TEN

Sometimes Chris thinks that it's all about food—home and family are.

He works to put food on the table. In the mornings Belle will have breakfast ready when the kids get up and an hour after that, their lunches packed for school. When he comes home from work there'll be food by six o'clock. The house always smells of food. Or baking. Belle hasn't inherited much from her parents' freak accident—*her father sober, always sober, but the highway slick with icy rain*—but she's inherited her mother's talent for baking. Corn bread. Banana bread. Cakes and pies.

She'd come in third in last year's county fair with the blueberry.

Today it's the corn bread. He can smell it riding high over the pot roast as soon as he walks in the door. He loves Belle's corn bread.

Brian is sprawled on the sofa watching some old Clint Eastwood movie on the forty-two-inch flat screen. Chris pops the clip in the Springfield and hands it to him.

"One shy," he says.

"I heard. Whatcha shootin' at, Pop?"

"You'll see."

He watches the movie for a minute. Eastwood is preparing a prison break. Brian goes to the cabinet, pulls out the box of shells and puts a fresh shell in the clip, then hands it back to him. He inserts the clip, safeties the weapon and stuffs it back into his jeans. He walks into the kitchen. And there on the table is the corn bread. He doesn't know how Peggy and Darlin' have resisted it, sitting right there in front of them. Peg is helping her sister with some sort of puzzle. He isn't even about to try to resist. He lifts up a square and bites.

Warm, delicious.

"You'll spoil your dinner," Belle says. She's stirring the gravy in the pot roast.

"Not a chance," he says.

"You say that now."

"I certainly do."

He sees her glance at his finger again, the gauze and pads brown at the tip. He's already been through the questions with her and the kids and told them basically nothing. *I had a little accident with a new project of mine. No big deal.* Luckily nobody has been around to actually see the damn thing while he treated it. They're women after all. He wouldn't have been surprised if one of them had fainted dead away.

He'll see Doc Richardson tomorrow. Get a shot or whatever.

God knows what's been in that mouth of hers.

He finishes the corn bread and licks his fingers.

"All right. Everybody want to come on down to the cellar with me?"

"Again?" Peggy says.

"Again at *dinnertime?*" says his wife.

"It's pot roast, Belle. Put it on simmer. You need to see this."

She looks at him a moment, then sighs and wipes her hands on a dishtowel and gives him a small, tolerant smile.

"Come on, girls. Do as your father says."

They are downstairs. Assembled. Standing at the foot of the stairs. Peggy and Darlin' holding hands. Brian with his mouth agape. Brian has been the first one down, all excited. As they crossed the lawn he asked, whatcha got in there, dad? A mountain lion? He was kidding of course and Cleek had acknowledged the fact with a grin.

A hellova lot more interesting than a mountain lion, son, he said. So now Brian stands there beside him. And his father is right. This is much more interesting than any cat.

Brian sees . . .

. . . his first half-naked woman, ever. There is more to his response than that because Brian is a complex young man but that's the first thing and it's primal. His eyes can barely leave her breasts to take in the rest of her—the bloody face, the matted hair. The fact that she is chained and helpless is not lost on him. Nor is the sheer size of her. But he has never seen Peg's breasts and his mother's he doesn't remember. He feels the beating of his heart. He feels a tremor.

And Peggy sees . . .

. . . a woman chained to a wall. Somebody has hurt her and that somebody is probably her father. She's been badly beaten. Her mouth is bloody and blood drools out her ear. It occurs to her to wonder how the woman has come to this. She's big and strong-looking and should have resisted. She is impressed by a kind of stillness about her, a silent watchfulness—but the woman also frightens her. Her smell frightens her. Her filth frightens her. What has her father done? How crazy is this? And how can she, Peg, go on living in this fucking house?

And Belle sees . . .

. . . wrongness, *evil.* In the size of her and the wildness in her which she can read plain like her mother used to read the palms of hands at parties and in her stink and her scars she sees what no woman should ever become, what no human should ever become. Chris Cleek doesn't believe in god or the devil, only pretends to believe. But she does and she's facing a devil of some kind for sure and she feels an almost pleasant thrill of terror that somehow this will get way out of control, chains or no chains, she can feel control slipping away even as she stands here—and then so sad suddenly for Chris and herself and her family and the life they're living now that she could almost cry. Instead she steels herself. Against whatever is to come.

And Darlin' . . . *Darleen* sees . . .

. . . a lady out of a picture book, out of a fairy tale where ladies are trapped in towers or given poison apples or like that movie where that lady is tied to two poles to wait for the great big ape, not a nice kind of fairy tale but the kind that makes you want to cry at first but then they're okay at the end and the lady comes down from the tower and the prince wakes her up and the ape dies. Except that the ape dying is kind of sad too. And the lady here smells like an ape, or what she thinks an ape would smell like if she ever saw one. The lady makes her nose itch.

And the Woman sees . . .

. . . a family. What the man has. And she has not.

ELEVEN

His children and Belle—at some point they each look at him, the father, for instruction. But it's Peggy who actually asks the question.

"Dad? What the hell is going *on* here?"

He pardons the swearing.

"God knows where she's been living, Peg. In the woods. In caves. We're going to help her."

"Help her? By chaining her up in a fruit cellar?"

He sees Belle shoot his daughter a warning glance. Good. Belle's standing by her man. Though he can see she's pretty damn puzzled too.

"She needs a big Band-Aid," Darlin' says. *Bless her.*

He smiles. "That's the first thing we're going to fix. She's been wounded. We'll get right to it. Okay, now listen. We're each going to share in the responsibility of taking care of her."

"The *police* should be taking care of her," Peggy says. "Or a hospital."

"No police. No hospitals."

"She's not some fucking *pet*, dad!"

"Peggy," says Belle, "you watch your mouth."

He lets that one pass too.

"The first rule, ground rule number one," he says, "is no touching."

He holds up his ruined finger, wiggles it. Darlin' giggles.

"I learned that the hard way. Our friend here likes to bite."

"She bit you?" says Belle.

"Took about an inch off my finger. Swallowed it."

"Jeez!" Brian's impressed. Well, he would be. Hell, *he's* impressed. If not in a good way.

"What are we going to do with her?" his son says.

"Train her, Brian. Civilize her. Free her from herself, her baser instincts. What we have here is . . . well, I've never seen anything quite exactly like it. This woman thinks she's an animal. Damned if I know how she got that way. But we can't have people running around in the woods thinking they're animals. It's not right. It's not safe."

He takes a quick survey of his family. Darlin's easy to read—Darlin's fascinated. Brian's probably thinking, *awesome.* Peggy is going to be trouble. Her face reads a mix of disbelief and disgust . . . or is that *contempt?* It better not be contempt. Belle is wearing that guarded look she has. The jury's still out with Belle. But she'll come around. She always does.

"Belle, why don't you run on up and put together a bowl of cereal or oatmeal or something. Something simple. The woman's got to be hungry. All she's had to eat since I found her is . . ."

He wags his finger again. Gets another giggle out of Darlin'.

"And Peg? Dig out the first-aid kit for me. I want to see to her wounds. Go on now, get a move on, ladies."

They both seem to hesitate for a moment and then Belle leads them up the stairs. Darlin' doesn't want to leave, he can tell, but Peg takes her hand and off they go. That leaves Brian standing there with him. The boy can't take his eyes off her. And that would figure too. She's a mess but she's still a woman full-grown and mostly naked. He can't help but smile.

"Better than a mountain lion, son?"

"Boy, you said it. Do we really get to keep her?"

"We do. Go out to the barn. Grab me a bow rake, will you?"

"Sure, dad."

He takes the stairs two at a time—and once out there, sets the dogs to barking. Have they been fed tonight? Probably. Who knows. He's tired of asking.

***

The man has done her a service. She doesn't know why. He has removed the poultices at her side, cleaned her wounds and replaced the poultices with ones of his own making, white. No, he has done her two services. He has removed the piss bowl from under her and used a crank on the wall to lower her down and allow her to rest on her knees, taking the strain from her arms and legs.

The man's family stands around him. His woman holds another bowl, smaller. The woman wears a worried look. But it is the younger one who interests her. She is perhaps the age of Second Stolen, a woman only beginning to be a woman. She seemed unwell at first but now she isn't sure. The Woman wonders if this is the man's birth daughter or if he has stolen her. She holds tight to the hand of the little girl.

The boy holds a rake with long light tines. She wonders if he means to stab her with it. She wouldn't be surprised.

The boy favors his father.

"Now, I can't stress this enough," Cleek says. "For the moment you keep your distance. So Belle, set the bowl down in front of her but not too close. And Brian, you push it forward with the rake so she can get at it. Careful not to spill it now. What'd you make her, Belle, oatmeal?"

"Yes."

"Good. Nice and nutritious. Go ahead and set it down."

She does.

"Brian?"

He moves it to within inches of her with the rake.

"There you go," Cleek says. "Teamwork. See? We all pitch in."

The woman doesn't seem to understand what this is all about at first.

And then she does.

***

They have given her a kind of gray-brown slop to eat which has no smell or smells of dust at best. And she is meant to put her face to this slop and lap it like a dog.

She is not a dog. But she can show them what a dog can do.

She growls, slams her forehead down onto the bowl, which shatters beneath the force of her.

Damn! Cleek thinks. Damned if she hasn't done it again!

Astonished him.

Darlin' lets out a little cry. The woman's scared the cry out of her. She's scared the whole damn family.

"You see what I mean about keeping your distance," he says. "I guess we just use plastic next time."

He takes the rake that Brian's gripping for dear life away from him and pushes the mess of oatmeal and crockery into a small pile in front of her.

"She gets hungry enough," he says, "she'll eat."

He gives the rake back to Brian and turns to his family.

"Now this is our project and it's a secret one. I shouldn't have to tell you to keep your mouths zipped but I'm telling you anyway. Each of us is gonna have chores with this one. Same as taking care of the dogs. Someone's got to pick up after her and so on. Your mother and I will take care of anything . . . overly complicated. Right, hon?"

Belle gives him a nod and a little smile. She doesn't like this at all, he can tell. But she'll do as she's told. They all will.

"All right," he says, "dinnertime. She may not be hungry but I sure am. We'll lay out the routine afterwards. Everybody okay with that?"

His tone says *do not fuck with me.*

Even Peggy nods.

Twelve

Peggy had halfway expected it, this little foray into her room tonight. Her father stood backlit by the hall light in the doorway gazing first at Darlin' asleep by the window and then at her. He walked over and sat down beside her on the bed.

"Everything okay at school?" he said.

"Sure, daddy."

It wasn't. But that was what he expected to hear, so that was what he got. She wondered if he detected the lie but simply ignored it. He was easily capable of that.

"You're a good girl, Peg. I know it's hard being your age sometimes but you've got to remember to look on the bright side. You'll have your license soon, right? Your grades are good. You'll be going to college. Think about that."

"Okay, dad."

College was all she *did* think about. Getting out of here.

And now with this new insanity . . .

It was as though he could read her thoughts. It wasn't the first time.

"I know you're upset about this woman. Don't be. We're doing her a mitzvah, Peggy, that's what the Jews say. A blessing. You'll see."

He smiled, put his arm over her shoulder, leaned down slowly and kissed her on the forehead, then gave her arm a gentle squeeze.

"Love you, kiddo," he said.

"Love you too, daddy."

It was their nightly mantra. Daddy and his kiddo. Their stupid, stupid call-and-response. Ever since she was a little girl.

She had grown to loathe it but there it was sometimes, even now after all these years. Yet another thing that trapped her.

He got off the bed and turned and she saw that her mother was standing in the hallway behind him. Watching.

All her mother ever seemed to do these days was watch.

She wondered if she'd always been like that, and that Peggy as a child just had never noticed. And if her mother had been that passive at her own age, when she and her father first met in the same high school corridor she now walked every day, or if it had happened gradually over time, this slippage—and if so, would it happen to her too someday. Would she inherit this. And gradually melt into the ghost of some unknown man's desires.

She was afraid it would. But then for a while she'd been afraid of a lot of things.

He showed no signs of displeasure at her being there watching them and Belle thought that was good—because she needed to try to have a serious discussion with him. In fact he placed a tender hand on the nape of her neck as they walked together to their room.

Once inside she turned on the bedside lamp and he closed the door and started to undress unbuttoning his shirt first the way he always did, his back to her as she put her hand to his shoulder. She warned herself against seeming too concerned.

"Chris, honey? Could we talk a minute? That woman. Do you really think we should be . . ."

He whirled and her hand dropped away from his shoulder and suddenly her face felt on fire.

He raised his other hand as though to slap her again. His eyes were glittering slits, his lips thinned, jaw set.

"Jesus, Chris!"

He let the hand fall slowly to his side.

He hadn't hit her since the abortion, what she thought of as the abortion though there had been no doctors involved, no clinics, no lines of protesters thank god. He hadn't hit her since. But even then he'd had no cause. She'd only said there were other ways to go about this than the one he proposed.

Her face stung and her ears rang.

You bastard, she wanted to say. *You son of a bitch.*

I didn't deserve that.

He turned and slipped out of his shirt, kicked out of his slippers, unbuttoned his pants and pulled them off his legs and folded both shirt and pants neatly over the corner chair. Then he sat down and patted the bed beside him. Smiled at her.

"Let's get some sleep, Belle."

He shifted to his side of the bed. Plumped the pillows. Pulled the covers over him. And then he was just lying there.

She took her own sweet time undressing and getting into her nightgown, sitting in front of the mirror and brushing out her hair. The woman looking back at her in the mirror wouldn't just fall asleep. Not tonight. Not for a long while.

She thought, if I had known back then, would I still have married him?

She had a lot of questions about herself. Always had. But she knew the answer to that one.

Brian listened in the dark for the house to settle. For everyone to sleep.

When he felt sure they had, he got out of bed and walked to the window opposite and as quietly as he could, raised the blinds. The yard was silent. No dogs barking or howling. No sound of night birds. Not even crickets. Down by the pond there would be crickets—and frogs too. But here? Nothing. Moonlight and stillness.

He stared at the fruit cellar door.

Stillness there too.

He wondered what she was doing down there. What she looked like hanging there in the dark. He imagined her in the dark.

She gazes at the mess of food and glass in front of her. She has bled from her ear into the food. It is easily within reach. She will not touch it.

She hears movement to her right, faint, from beneath the old trunk across the room. She has no need to scent the air to know what makes these sounds. The scent has been with her for a long time. The scratching sounds are mice and she sees them now, three of them, hesitant yet scurrying toward her in short fits and starts.

Three small brown mice who at last find the food in front of her and do what she will not.

PART TWO

Thirteen

The morning was bright, a crisp in the air before the day's heat took hold. He drove to work with the windows open and took his time along the coast roads. They made him think of her and where she'd been—without the Quickie Marts and Robin's Donuts or Captain Submarines along the way to distract him. He thought of her wandering along the Canadian shoreline. All the time alone.

He could make the drive from his house to work in half an hour but today it took him three-quarters of an hour before he passed the Coast Tide Inn and the Old Curiosity Shoppe and then the library and courthouse into the center of town. He parked the Escalade in his usual spot in front of Apple Tree Books and climbed the single flight of stairs to his office above.

Betty of course was already at her computer. She wore that pretty green sleeveless dress she knew he liked that went so well with her curly red hair. She greeted him with her usual smile and a *good morning, Mr. Cleek.* Twenty-one and eager and sweet as sugar.

"Mornin', Betty. How'd things go with Mrs. Oldenberg? She satisfied with the papers?"

"Didn't even read them. Signed them right away."

"Fine. Though I always counsel against that."

She looked at her desk calendar.

"You've got lunch with Dean at noon. Then court at two and a meeting with those Exxon reps at three thirty. Are they really going to tear down McAllen's Hardware?"

"Not if the town council and I can help it. Last thing we need is a gas station three blocks away from the Royal Bank of Canada. Those DeFuria files ready?"

"I just have to print out this last one."

"Well, bring 'em on in when you're done along with a cup of mud and we'll get to it. Thanks, Betty."

Betty had this sort of funny tic, this habit. Whenever she turned back to her computer from talking to him or somebody else, as she did now, she took a deep breath as though about to take an underwater plunge. Which had the effect of plumping out those more-than-sufficient breasts against whatever she was wearing.

He'd considered what those breasts would be like *without* whatever she was wearing more than once. But he was a lawyer after all and she a paralegal and they both knew all about harassment suits and the workplace. He was pretty sure Betty had a crush on him. But still.

Maybe someday he'd find reason to fire her. But gently. It would have to be something that would sit well with her. Maybe some big client would bitterly complain. And then what could a guy do? *My god, sorry, Betty, but you know these big-money boys. They always get their way.*

She was pretty good at her job though. Be a shame to lose her. But you never could tell.

Peg watched her class do stretches on the field. The bleachers were hard on your butt but it was better than being out there.

Mrs. Jennings' whistle shrilled. So loud that Dee Dee Hardcoff covered her ears. Peg hated that damn whistle—all of them did. The girls filed in across the track. Her teacher wore the high school colors. Green shorts, white blouse. She had no breasts at all to speak of and short stocky legs and walked like a man. Peggy wondered if she was gay. She was married but that didn't mean a lot these days.

"Okay, eight laps, ladies."

There went the whistle again. The girls seemed to heave a collective sigh and started in to trot. Mrs. Jennings saw her sitting there and walked over.

"Peg? Not feeling well again today?"

Well obviously, she wanted to say. She didn't like the woman's tone of voice at all. It was just this bit shy of sarcastic, just this bit shy of accusatory. But teachers didn't have to give a shit about their tone of voice, did they.

"No. Not too well."

"See your pass?"

She dug into her backpack for the note from the nurse's office. Handed it over.

The woman seemed to study it forever—as though looking for flaws. *Could the bitch even read?* Did gym teachers have to pass basic English? She handed back the note and nodded and walked back to the field without a word.

Well that was nice, she thought, and fuck you very much.

Back behind the ticket booth Genevieve Raton was sharing Marlboros with Bill Fulmer. Fulmer taught shop. He was in his forties, married, with two kids, short and plump and balding. He knew his way around a lathe or circular saw and was without the slightest hint of the teacherly arrogance she saw in a lot of in the tenured staff here and Genevieve liked him a lot.

"So this is your spot, huh?" she said.

In the teachers' lounge she'd said she was dying for a smoke. But smoking had been banned from the lounge twenty years ago as with everywhere else in or around the school. Usually she just left her pack in the glove compartment and suffered in silence until the bell rang and the day was over. But today Bill had said, *come with me.*

The ticket booth was perfect. The back door was the entrance directly to the gym. Nobody used it but the gym classes. Once they were out on the field you could only be seen from the parking lot. And during the school day nobody used that either.

"Been sneaking back here on my breaks for years now," Fulmer said. "Smoke-free campus, my ass. All you have to do is police your butts."

"You're a genius, Bill. I think we'll be running into one another more often from now on."

He smiled and nodded. "Always glad of the company, Ms. Raton."

She glanced around the corner at the field. Saw Peggy Cleek sitting alone in the bleachers, her arms crossed over her lap, using her backpack for a pillow.

"You know Peggy Cleek, Bill? That girl over there?"

"Can't say I do. Why?"

"There's something going on with her. The last month or so she's changed. A lot."

"They do at that age, Genevieve. And fast."

"I know. But this is . . . you know how they're all dressing these days. The shorter the skirt the better, the skimpier and tighter the blouses and tees. Well, that's how she was too. Now it's all sweats and hoodies that are way too big for her. And don't think the other kids aren't noticing. They're giving her funny looks. She's a very pretty girl. She ought to be . . ."

"Flaunting it?"

"Yeah. Dammit. Flaunting it."

They laughed.

"Did you, at her age, Genevieve? Flaunt it?"

He wasn't coming on to her—he knew her better than that. He was teasing. She figured she could tease right back.

"I'd have made you pop your fucking zipper, William."

Belle knew the IGA like the back of her hand and so did Darlin' by now. She also knew that her daughter was bored to death with marketing and she had a window of about fifteen minutes before the whining started. She was too old to ride in the cart anymore and too young to leave on her own at home after Kindervale school—and Chris wouldn't hear of hiring a sitter. So she paused only briefly over the cuts of pork loin and bottom round and otherwise moved them along through the aisles as quickly as possible.

Between the Arm & Hammer laundry detergent and the Lava soap she saw Vickie Silverman headed her way, smiling, her two-year-old Bennie's legs jiggling out of the cart basket. She put on her own smile and reached for the Lava.

"Hi, Belle. Hi, Darlin'. And how are you two today?" Vicki was a cheek-pincher. Darlin' was well aware of that and kept her distance.

"We're fine, Vic. And you?"

"All's well here. We measured Bennie this morning and he's grown another half inch! How about that. What do you think? Barbecue again soon?"

"I don't see why not. Weather's been perfect for it, hasn't it."

"Your place this time, maybe?"

Her voice said *finally? Good god,* she thought. *That's all I need. And aren't you being a little forward volunteering me, Vicki? Even if we haven't had guests over for barbecue in god knows how many years?*

"Oh, I don't know, the place is just such a darn mess."

"With little ones around, how can it ever *not* be?"

"You're right about that. But the big ones don't help much either. I've got to run, Vic. See you soon, okay?"

"Of course. See you soon."

They moved their separate ways up and down the aisle.

Guests, she thought. Children. Running all over the place. The barn. The fruit cellar. That'll be the day.

He handed Betty his notes out of the briefcase. He used his good hand.

"Okay," he said. "Here are the basics of our agreement. All the figures and dates of payment spelled out for you. Standard purchase agreement form. When you're finished, send 'em over to Dean for signature along with the initial check. And send him a case of Dewar's while you're at it."

Betty nodded but then just stood there a moment in front of his desk.

"Mr. Cleek? May I say something?"

"Of course, Betty. What is it?"

He wondered if she knew how cute she looked when her brow got all furrowed like that.

"It's none of my business, really. But in this economy, are you sure you aren't . . ."

"Overextending?"

He'd considered it. If some downturn in his stocks hit him bigtime or if somebody in his family got seriously ill he could be in a bit of trouble here. It was possible. Betty probably knew his finances better than Belle did, so he could understand her concern. But Dean's asking price was ridiculously low.

Well, it had *gotten* ridiculously low after their little chat over lunch today.

"I'm sure, Betty. Don't you worry. That's a nice perfume by the way. New, is it?"

She was cute when she blushed too.

"You like it?"

"It's very nice."

"Thanks!"

It was then that she finally noticed the bandage. Hell it was a big bandage. She reached out for his hand.

"What in the lord's name did you do to yourself, Mr. Cleek?"

Her hands were very soft and smooth. Then she seemed to realize she'd committed a tiny little indiscretion here. She released him.

He held up his finger as though inspecting it.

"Got too close to a pretty-smelling lady and she just . . ."

He snapped his teeth together. *Chomp.*

Betty laughed, shook her head at him as if to say, *you big kidder, you* and turned to walk away.

Hide in plain sight, his father used to say.

Well, some things, anyway.

Fourteen

There were times Belle thought her daughter acted like a little puppy and this was one of them, Darlin' standing right beside her hip, impatient as a puppy at feeding time while she whipped the cookie batter. She turned off the mixer and tilted back the beaters and then decided to tease her.

She unlocked one of the beaters and tapped it on the bowl. Then ran a finger along one side. Tasted it. *Mmmmmm,* she said.

"Hey!"

"What?"

"Gimme some!"

"Now is that a nice way to ask?"

"Please, momma? I love you!"

"That's much better."

She leaned over and gave her a kiss on the cheek and handed her the beater. Darlin' sat down and went to work.

"Can we make the little men?"

She pulled a cookie cutter out of the drawer. An elephant.

"This one?"

"No."

A dinosaur next. "This one?"

"No."

Then a bird. "How about this one?"

"Noooooooo!"

And finally the one she wanted all along. The gingerbread man. Even if they were vanilla cookies.

"Yes!"

Darlin' fished the last of the cookie batter off the beater with the tip of her pinky.

"Do you think that animal lady will eat a little man?"

"I don't know. I don't know if she's ever had a cookie before."

"Why's the lady here?"

"Papa's helping her. You heard him."

"Can I have the other one now?"

"Sure, honey."

She tapped the second beater free of loose batter and handed it to her daughter. Conversation closed. She thought, well, that was easy.

In the morning the man has removed the broken bowl and what little the mice have left behind and hauled her upright again. There is very little slack but some. She works her wrists back and forth trying to loosen the bolts but they have remained solid and unyielding and she has been at this all day, so that her wrists are raw. She has tried steady pressure. She has tried sudden jerks. All she has attained are bleeding wrists. She accepts the pain and tries again.

She senses something and stops, listens. There is someone at the door. The sliver of afternoon sunlight at the bottom of the door flickers with movement. She scents the air.

It is not the man. The man wears a scent of flowers and musk. She stands silent and a moment passes. No one enters. Then she hears voices, the woman's voice far away and angry—and then the boy's voice, defensive, just outside the door.

She thinks she knows why he has been here.

"Brian! Young man? What do you think you're doing!"

He turned to face his mom all hot and bothered standing on the porch with his sister.

"I was just trying to see if she was okay."

"That what you want me to tell your father? Get over here. Right now."

Hell, it was a disappointment anyhow. He'd gotten off the bus and made record time up the driveway to the fruit cellar but once he got there he found that the door was hung too true against its frame to provide a spot to see through. What he needed was a knothole or something. There wasn't one.

He stood up and snagged his shoulder bag and trudged to the house.

His sister bit an arm off a headless cookie.

"Want a little man?"

She offered him one. His mother was still glowering at him with her arms folded across her chest like some guy in the military but his sister seemed pretty much oblivious to that. He took the cookie, placed it flat in the palm of his hand and gave it a karate chop with the other.

"Hey," said Darlin', "you're supposed to eat the head first!"

"Not me. I chop 'em. Thanks, sis."

He walked past them through the screen door his mom held open for him and headed upstairs to his room.

Not a bad cookie. He bit off a leg and chewed.

They were headed home in the Escalade and as usual her father was on the cell phone.

"Hell, Dean, I hated to have to write a check that cost me a good neighbor but if someone had to, glad to be of service. Sure. Sure. Think nothing of it. I'd be happy to help you through one of those bottles but I've got a family thing at home tonight. 'Nother time, right? Good man. Okay, I'll be talking to you. See ya, Dean."

He snapped the phone shut.

Her father looked very pleased with himself, she thought. She didn't need to know why.

He reached into his coat pocket and took out a pack of Winstons and his lighter. Shook one free and lit up. Smoke drifted her way.

"Dad? Could you not? I mean, I don't think it's good . . ."

He shot her a look. But then hit the console button and rolled down the window and flicked the damn thing out. She'd won that one at least.

"Better?" he said.

"Better."

When Brian saw them pull in he was off the porch before they got the car doors open, wearing his most ingratiating smile. Peg would see through it. Dad wouldn't. And it was dad he needed to please just in case his mother mentioned that fruit cellar shit.

As ever the past few years since he turned thirteen, dad offered his hand. He looked to be in a real good mood. *Excellent.* They shook hands.

"Don't forget the dogs," he said to Peg. They were already barking.

"It's Brian's turn."

She moved past them toward the porch. She *didn't* look to be in a real good mood. Tough shit.

"Brian?"

"On it!" he said.

What he thought was, *fucking dogs.*

He walked to the barn and slid open the door and the dogs set to barking like he was some fucking ax murderer come to chop the shit out of them. The dogs didn't like Brian any more than he liked them—they weren't so nuts about his father either as a matter of fact. Particularly Agnes, the mother, who would get so worked up she'd take a nip out of George and Lily, born of her own litter. The other two dogs gave her plenty of personal space. Just like they were doing now. They just stood off together to one side of the cage, her on the other, in front of the doghouse, making one hell of a racket, barking and growling.

"Oh shut up, assholes!"

But they weren't about to.

He was supposed to hose down the food bowls and the water bowls outside the cage but nobody was going to notice if he didn't. So instead what he did was, he grabbed the hose off its hook. They were afraid of that. They backed off a little when he opened the cage door. He pointed the nozzle at them like he was going to use it on them and they backed off further. He squirted some water into each of the water dishes and then picked up the food dishes and shut the cage door and filled them with kibble and brought them back inside.

He set down the dish in front of the doghouse and Agnes growled and then had the balls to actually snap at him. *Once.* He pointed the hose at her. For a moment they were eye to eye.

"You better cut that out, bitch," he said. "You want the hose? You want the fuckin' hose?"

She didn't. The dog blinked and the fight went out of her eyes. The moment passed. He'd won again, he thought. He always won. Agnes went back to her own dish and started slobbering away. Brian bent down low and peered inside the doghouse. *This* one he hardly ever saw. Probably scared of Agnes too.

"Where's the baby?" he said. "Where's the baby? She sleepin'?"

It was dark in there but he could just see the outline of her and saw the old checkered blanket move a bit. He could hear her panting.

He figured she'd either come out when he left to get her food or else she wouldn't. Didn't matter to him either way. He'd give it one last try though. He liked watching her eat.

"C'mon, girl. You gonna have some food, baby?"

He thought later that the low growl should have warned him off but it didn't. So that when the lunge came and the teeth snapped just inches from his goddamn face he fell back onto his ass and scraped his hands against rough concrete and something else—something hard at first and then crumbling soft against his left palm.

Dog shit. Jeezus.

"You little son of a bitch!" he said.

He'd like to have beat the shit out of her. But he was pretty damn quick to get out of there instead.

Belle watched him get out of his dress shirt and slacks and handed him some cutoffs and a work shirt.

"Signed and sealed," he said. "Not another resident within three miles now."

"Well, you finally have your own little country, don't you?"

She was remembering that slap last night. Still the sarcasm wasn't like her. Not with him. But he didn't seem to notice.

"My question is, can we really afford it, Chris?"

"Of course we can. Everything quiet around here today?"

"I haven't heard a thing."

"You look in on her?"

"No. Why would I?"

He ignored that too. Slipped into his work shirt.

"Go down and boil some water for those buckets, Belle, okay? Let's get to it."

By the time Cleek got his shoes on and came downstairs she was already at the gas stove firing up two big chili-pots full of water. Darlin' was at the kitchen table, a plate of cookies shaped like little men in front of her. She was messing with two of them—walking them around, making them jump, flip, zoom across the table. He considered telling her not to play with her food but decided to hell with it, let it go. Peg sat across from her reading a magazine. He could hear something tinny from her iPod. Which meant it was turned up loud.

Brian walked in looking kind of flustered.

"You feed the dogs?"

"Yeah."

"I need you to go out there again. Get the pooper-scooper off the beam and bring it in here. Brian? I smell something."

Brian looked down at his hand.

"I thought I had it hosed all off of me. I slipped and fell into some dog turds."

"Well, go wash your hands for godsakes. Then get me that scooper."

Darlin' made believe that she was the animal woman. She was the animal woman and the men were all running away from her but she was bigger and faster and *rawr!* she said and grabbed one up and the little man looked at her and said *noooooo! Noooooo! Don't eat meeeeeee!*

She bit his head off anyway.

He pulled the scoop off the beam and noticed on the shelf beside it his father's old hand-crank drill. His father had an electric drill now of course but it was his habit to save everything whether it was going to be used again or not.

Brian thought he might have a very good use for it indeed.

He popped a stick of Wrigley's in his mouth.

He worked fast and hard too because it was more difficult than he might have guessed to get the thing through three-quarters of an inch of weathered wood and he was nervous as hell because if somebody glanced out the window and saw him out here doing this there was going to be big trouble. But in a while that seemed like a long while he had a hole drilled at the bottom left-hand corner of the door about two feet above the base. He brushed off the shavings and got down and had a look.

At first all he saw were her legs, dim in the darkness of the cellar. Then he adjusted his position. He saw her thighs, her belly streaked with grime, her breasts. He blinked and looked up again and saw her face and rolled away onto his back as though struck by sudden lightning.

She was staring straight at him.

He could feel his face flush, the pulse pounding in his forehead.

Easy, he thought. Calm down, kiddo.

He took out the wad of gum and rolled it in the dirt until it was completely covered and plugged the hole and then smoothed it over with his hand. Looked good—the same brown color as the door. He stood up and dusted off his ass, grabbed the scoop and drill and raced back to the barn, dropped the drill on its shelf and walked back to the house all laid-back and casual.

His mother was carefully dumping boiling water from the chili pots into a pair of wash buckets. His father was reading his paper.

"Where you been?" he said.

"I was playing around with the dogs a little."

His father put the paper down.

"You?" he said.

"Yeah. I do, sometimes."

His father shrugged, then stood.

"We ready, Belle?"

"We're ready."

"All right then. Brian, take a bucket. Careful not to spill."

"Yessir."

And that was it. He'd gotten over.

FIFTEEN

Light pours through the musty room, and wind. She is grateful for the breeze and the scent of land and living things. For a moment she is blinded again to all but the dust motes swirling in front of her. She sees the figure above like a black ghost that gradually resolves itself into the man, her captor, descending the stairs.

She braces herself. For anything.

"How we doin' today?" he says and sets the towels and dishrags and Lava soap down beside the winch.

"Sorry about this. But with you I'm taking no more chances."

He cranks the winch. One turn, two. He knows this is uncomfortably tight now, can see the pull in the tendons of her arms and thighs. But it's necessary. The woman makes no sound of complaint, not even a grunt. Again he admires her. Tough bitch, this one is.

He gives the winch one more turn.

And she can feel the bolt at her right wrist give slightly. The man has done damage to his own handiwork. Not enough damage, not yet. But some. Her wrists are oozing blood but when the boy and the woman walk down the stairs to join him he turns his back to her for a moment and she works the wrist as best she can.

Belle and Brian set the buckets of steaming hot water down on the cellar floor.

"The scooper, Brian."

"Right. Forgot."

The kid takes the stairs two at a time. He knows his son's enjoying this. Let him. His son's practically a man.

He unwraps the bar of soap, folds it into a dishrag and dips it into the water. Damn! *That shit's hot!* It practically burns his fingers. He works it into a lather experimentally as Brian bolts back down the stairs with the scooper. Thinks, this'll work just fine.

"Gonna scrub her down, pop? I never seen anybody—*smelled* anybody—that nasty before! Jeez!"

His son is grinning.

"Your mother and I are. But first you need to clean up her mess."

"Me?"

"Yes, Brian. You."

The grin's disappeared now. Cleek doesn't blame the boy. It's not a job anybody'd want. She's missed the Tupperware bowl entirely with her shit though most of her piss is in there.

"Use the scooper and one of these rags here. We'll just have to clean up after her until we get her . . ."

"Potty trained?"

The grin is back again. His son is nothing if not resilient.

"Exactly."

Brian sets to. And it's not lost on him that the boy is concentrating on those long firm legs as much as he is on the job he's doing. Brian points to what's left of the food and the food bowl.

"This too?"

"Yeah. Let her think on eating for a while."

When he's done he just stands there, scooper in hand.

"Okay, now get."

"But I can help you . . ."

He gives his son a look. It's a look that's always stopped him dead in his tracks and today is no exception. Fun is fun but he's not about to let his boy wash down a full-grown woman. Brian sighs and trudges up the stairs.

"And close the door behind you."

Cleek turns on the overhead light and snaps on a pair of rubber work gloves. The cellar door slams shut.

Belle's standing behind him, twisting nervously at her wedding ring.

"You might want to take that off," he says. "And put on a pair of these. This is going to be messy."

He watches her work the ring off her finger and shove it in the pocket of her Bermudas. It occurs to him that all this time down here Belle hasn't yet said a word. He's guessing she's not too sanguine about all this. He wishes she were but he knows his wife. She's always been a timid thing. When they met as kids that was attractive to him. It's not anymore.

She puts on the rubber gloves.

"Grab a bucket."

They move to within about three feet of the woman and set down the buckets. He dips the soapy dishrag into the steaming water, lathers it up more and presses it to the woman's forehead and

she smells it long before it touches her, a disgusting mix of fats and other scents not of her world and when it touches her she can feel her skin crawl beneath the hot cloth and bastard! son of a whore! *she screams and tears at the shackles holding her, every muscle in her body working to get to him and tear at him screaming all the while as he stumbles back and*

kicks the pail at Belle's feet, which nearly overturns, sloshes steaming water all over his wife's bare legs so that she screams and the woman is screaming at him too *"Bastart! Mac dar striapach!"* over and over, thrashing side to side and forward and back—he can hear her spine banging against the shelf behind her and the rage comes riding through him like a runaway train.

"That's how you want to play? Fine!"

He bends down and picks up the bucket at Belle's feet and flings its contents. The water that has scalded his poor wife's legs now leaps out of the bucket all over the woman's shoulder, her neck, her cheek, her belly. Her scream goes hoarse and guttural.

And abruptly, stops.

It burns! Hot enough to take her breath away.

The man picks up the second bucket. And she is immediately aware of two things simultaneously. The first gives her hope. The bolt to her right has loosened considerably. The second gives her shame. Because she knows that the look in her eyes has changed.

From a look of defiance to one of fear. Fear of that second bucket.

And knows he sees this too.

Brian sits at the screened window staring out toward the cellar. It isn't fair, he thinks. But then, when were adults ever fair? He jumps up at the sudden screaming outside coming from the cellar and heads for the door. No way he's missing this. Fuck it. Peg passes him in the hall. She's chomping on an apple.

"Hey! You're gonna catch hell if you go back down there, Bri," she says.

"Suck my dick, sis," he says.

He races outside.

"This what you want? You want more?"

And she gets his drift. He can tell she gets it. There's something in her eyes that's almost humble—almost pleading with him. He likes that. Likes it a lot. He wonders if she's ever looked at anybody that way before exactly and he likes that thought even better. That he should be the first.

He sets the bucket down.

He looks to his wife.

"You okay, honey?"

Her legs are splotched beet red. She hisses in a breath, speaks through gritted teeth.

"Yes."

"Good. Let's try this again."

She shakes her head like this is crazy which he doesn't much care for but unwraps her own bar of soap and folds it into a dishrag which he likes.

His mom and dad are standing in front of the woman with dishrags in their hands and he doesn't see what all the commotion was about. The woman seems calm enough. His view through the peephole is perfect but he can barely hear them through the door. He listens carefully. He doesn't want to miss a thing.

"Maybe we should let this cool down a bit before . . ." his mom says.

His father interrupts her. "Now, hon," he says, "you know as well as I do that the best way to get something clean is with good hot water. Might as well be shuffling germs around if we go cold or hell, even room temp. Remember, we're totally in control here."

His dad approaches the woman with the rag and squeezes some soapy water out over her head. It runs down her forehead and cheek and neck all the way down to her tits. Even from here he can see that her nipples are hard.

So is he.

The woman doesn't move. His dad is pleased.

"Good," he says.

He dips the rag into the water again and brings it to the woman's cheek and scrubs. Brian can see her wince at his touch.

"Look there. We got a clean spot."

His mother says something he can't quite hear.

The woman sneezes. The soap tickling her nose he guesses. Brian almost laughs out loud but he stifles that. She looks so miserable hanging there. He'd bet she's never had a proper civilized soap-and-water bath in all her life.

This is *awesome* fun.

His dad washes her other cheek. Her forehead, then her nose and chin and around her mouth. That's a little bit scary, this part. He remembers—and he knows his father sure as hell remembers—that she took off the tip of his finger just yesterday. She could easily take off another right now if she wanted to but she doesn't for some reason. Then he notices that the whole right side of her looks scalded. So that was what all the screaming was about.

His dad's tamed her. With scalding hot water. *Way to go, dad.*

The woman's face is still streaked but way cleaner and gleaming wet and bright from the heat. His mother's just standing there with the soapy rag in her hand, watching him. He wonders why she isn't helping. He sure would.

His father's dipped the rag again and gone on to her neck, front and back, scrubbing hard. The woman's glaring at him now. He doesn't seem to notice.

"Come on, Belle, give me a hand here."

His mother dips her rag in the water but that's all she does. It's as though she's afraid to move. But it's not that. He sees something in her posture that he's seen before—it's very familiar. Something his father also doesn't notice. His mother's angry. It's all bottled up inside her there but she's angry all right.

Dad's done with her neck. He's working on her shoulders. Getting closer and closer to . . .

. . . those amazing tits . . .

She has known for some time now. She has sensed it and there is no need to put it to the test. In the slightest movement of her hand inside the bolt she senses it.

***

"Don't you go getting all foolish on me, Belle," his father says. "It's just something's gotta be done."

Her shoulders are clean. He dips the rag into the water again.

He tries to hide it from his woman and perhaps he can but he cannot hide it from her. His heart is racing. His pulse pounding. He is focused on her breasts. He reaches out for them with the dripping cloth.

And the second he touches her, the second she feels the heat, she tears the bolt free of the wall and her hand darts to his neck like a striking snake and she is soaring, roaring with elation. Her fingers dig deep into the muscles of his neck and the man struggles, tries to pry her hand free but his two hands are not nearly a match for her single hand and the long-bred strength that resides there and she is grinning directly into his horror-struck face as he writhes and chokes and sees his death hovering in her eyes.

This is the pleasure of the hunt.

This is the will and the power and the freedom.

This is the joy of her creation.

He is going down beneath her grip.

Then the door is flung open and thunder booms.

He has raced back to the house for the gun and it's all a blur, one huge red blur—it seems only an instant later he's run past Peg and Darlin' standing in the hall with Peg saying *what??* and down the stairs and then he's there inside the cellar, first dimly aware of his father on his knees in front of her by now, his arms limp at his sides, the woman's hand clutching his neck and his mother simply standing there with her hands over her mouth and then the next thing he knows the .45 leaps in his own hands and a bullet ricochets off the back wall and the side wall and the stairway directly behind him.

And then he's in front of her pointing the gun right in her face and he hears himself say *back off!*

The woman hesitates, looks him in the eyes as though to verify his intent. And then drops his father gasping for breath to the cellar floor. His father is coughing violently. He can hear it over the gunshot ringing in his ears. He's aware of movement behind him and then a firm hand pushes him roughly aside.

He corrects his balance just in time to see his mother, lips pressed tight together, tears pooling in her eyes, whack the woman in the side of the head with a length of two-by-four. The woman goes slack.

The woman is out.

He realizes he's barely breathing. He hauls in a deep one.

His mother. Who'd have thought it?

It's ridiculous and yet not so ridiculous given the occasion but an old song lyric pops into his mind that his dad likes.

Stand by your man.

His mom tosses away the two-by-four clattering to the floor and goes to him. Helps him up.

"Thanks," he says. His voice is weak. His eyes all skittery. His hand is at his neck. He turns to Brian.

"Go get me a hammer and the drill, son," he says. "Need to drive a new one. Deeper. A lot deeper."

He reaches for the gun and Brian hands it over.

"Dad. I'm sorry. I know I'm not supposed to . . . but . . ."

"It's okay, boy. You did good. Real good. Now get me those tools, okay?"

And it stays with him, what his dad said, as he hits the stairs. *You did good. Real good.*

He has never quite gotten those words out of his father before. Not once. Never.

SIXTEEN

He can do this practically with his eyes closed as he can do most other things that require physical skill and dexterity but he's having trouble concentrating and he thinks that even Belle can see that, Belle standing to one side with the .45 to the woman's head by way of discouragement while he drives the eyebolt into a new hole which he means to get all the way down to the loop but he's missed the damn thing twice which is not like him at all.

His trouble is that he isn't quite sure why he's doing this. Why he doesn't just let her go to live out her miserable savage life however she sees fit. And this is not like him either, to be unsure. He's sure in his business and he's sure with his family and friends and acquaintances which is a better word actually because he has no close friends really, has never wanted them, has never trusted them. He trusts Belle and his kids and that's it. That's all he needs.

He's looked over the subject of why he's doing this and around and through the subject and he doesn't have an answer except that he wants to. He knows it's probably dangerous, forget the fact that physically she's one fucking dangerous beast, but if he wanted to count them he knows he's probably breaking a dozen laws or more, he's putting them all in a kind of jeopardy here but all he can come up with in terms of a *why* is that he wants to see this little experiment of his through to its fruition. Just as his cheerful sweet drunk of a mother used to call Chris her own little experiment meaning that she'd have one kid, sure, but no more, she'd never willingly birth another.

But he sees this wildness in her and it attracts him powerfully in both his dick and his brain, he knows that much and he does want to tame her, he does want to know if it's possible. He's tamed himself god knows. And if he could do that with the kid he was why not her? If he had the will and the strength to break himself like you'd break a crazy wild horse he ought to be able to do the same with her.

Maybe he has some kind of sister-in-spirit here, maybe that's it.

Maybe he sees something in her that he also sees in himself—only purer of purpose, sleeker in its aggressive design. He loves his own aggression. It's made him what he is today.

Maybe he's doing this because he loves himself. His pure self. The self without the makeover.

It's possible.

He hammers the bolt home.

SEVENTEEN

And there they were again today like any other day, all those dopey sweet hormone-driven bubblegum-popping teenage girls with their tight jeans and tight bottoms filing out of her classroom with sidelong glances at the boys—and she wished she'd looked like some of them at that age truth be told, it had taken her four years of aerobics and yoga and fat-burning and nickle-and-diming on her diet to get to where she was today. Which admittedly was pretty good. But still . . .

There they were, all those girls. And there was Peggy Cleek. Faded hoodie and sweatpants again. Posture all gone to hell just like some of the freshman girls who were trying to hide their new-blooming breasts, who didn't yet get what their assets were going to be.

Hiding.

It came to her all at once like some kind of Zen slap. She knew enough about how her particular brain worked to suspect that it had been forming for quite a while, an uneasy intuition. But now there it was.

"Can I talk to you for a minute, Peg?"

"I don't want to be late for next period, Ms. Raton."

"I'll write you a note. Sit down for a sec, would you?"

She sighed and sat, slumped forward. *Like she's trying to crawl into herself,* she thought. Genevieve sat at the desk in front of her, straddling the chair to face her. She studied the girl's face a moment and realized something.

She reminds me a little of Dorothy Burgess. My first.

It was sad how that had ended.

"You all right?" she said.

"I'm fine. Why?"

She smiled, trying to relax her. The girl was tight as a guitar string.

"How come you're dressing like this lately?"

She shrugged.

"I'm sorry, Peggy. But the only reason a girl your age would cover up this much is if she had something to cover up. You didn't until just recently."

"I don't get what you mean, Ms. Raton."

"Nausea. Baggy clothes. Mrs. Jennings tells me you've been sitting out gym for weeks now. Peg, I'm not stupid."

Though I have been, for not getting this sooner. That, and for not anticipating her reaction.

Defensive is what she'd expected. What she got was hostility.

"Why don't you mind your own business, Ms. Raton!"

Okay. She rolled with that one.

"You are my business," she said. "You're my student. You used to be one of my very best students. Who's the father?"

"Father? You're crazy!"

"I'd like to speak with your parents, Peg."

It was as though she'd smacked her across the face. She stood suddenly rigid at her desk and then took one step backward.

"No. Don't do that," she said. "Listen, I've got to get to class . . ."

She picked up her backpack and turned to go.

"Wait. Hold on. Let me write you that note."

She's trembling, she thought. Her whole body's trembling. *She's scared.*

Very scared.

Leave it go, Genevieve. Don't push her. At least not for now.

Still, she took her time walking back to her desk and even more time scribbling out the note to her teacher. She wanted to let the girl think about it for a moment or two. To let her calm down a bit. She shouldn't have to go to another class this way. It was possible she shouldn't have to go to another class at all.

"I'd like you to consider confiding in me, Peggy," she said. "It helps to have someone to talk to sometimes, you know?" She didn't answer. Genevieve hadn't expected her to. She handed her the note. The girl practically ran for the door.

She said, "Anytime you want."

Belle sat in the late-afternoon sunshine streaming through her living room window, feeding blue cotton fabric through her mother's old Singer, keeping a practiced even pressure on the pedal. Chris had wanted to buy her a Brother computerized-type model last Christmas but she'd said no, her mother's machine still worked just fine thank you very much. Bad enough there were already three computers in the house—one in Peg's room, one in Brian's room and one in Chris' study—and bad enough they each had cell phones too and a flat-screen Blu-ray TV that looked like something out of *Star Trek* and an answering machine with caller ID and call waiting. The modern age could stop at sewing.

Normally it was something she enjoyed. The last time she'd done any sewing was for Darleen's Halloween costume. Darleen wanted to be Peter Pan. They reminded her that Peter Pan was actually a little boy but she was adamant. So Peter Pan it was. And the *first* time she'd used her mother's machine was on the pattern for a wrap skirt for her sister Suzie when they were both just teenagers, Belle the elder by three years. Suzie had loved it. But her sister had moved to Dead River, Maine, and wasn't speaking to her anymore. Not for several months now. Not since Thanksgiving dinner down there when Chris, slightly in his cups, had insinuated that her husband Willie, a garage mechanic or *grease monkey* as he tended to put it, was a loser. He and Willie had almost come to blows. Well, Willie *was* a loser. But Chris didn't have to announce it over Thanksgiving dinner.

But today she wasn't enjoying sewing at all. It was the *why* of it.

The dress was simple, easy to make.

But the dress was for that woman.

Brian loved the power-sound of it. The hiss of water and the growl of the generator and now too the pounding against the plywood that reduced the dogs' frenzied barking to mere background noise. Paint chips flew off the old weathered board.

"Dial it down," his father said. "But not too much."

She hears a strange sound coming from outside or perhaps a mix of sounds none of which she understands except for the barking of the dogs. Her head is pounding. She pulls hard against her restraints but there is no give this time. She waits. There is nothing to do but wait.

She has learned patience on the hunt. And vigilance.

Eighteen

Cleek and Brian lug the generator down the stairs. Heavy sonovabitch, Brian thinks. Brian's got the top and most of the weight is at the bottom but even so. They set it down and his dad takes one more drag off the Winston dangling from his lips and tosses it away.

The woman's watching them. Giving them the evil eye.

"Make sure the extension's secure up there and then go inside and fetch your mom and Peg."

"Can't I help?"

"You helped plenty. Go on."

The woman's still glaring at them and his father's leaned down to flip the switch of the pressure washer's onboard storage tank of cleaning solution to the ON position so Brian takes that opportunity to pick up his dad's butt, still smoldering, and flick it at her. It hits her in the belly and sparks fly. He grins. She continues glaring. He gathers she doesn't like him. So what.

Inside the house mom's at the sewing machine.

"Dad's ready for you," he says.

"I'll be finished here in just a minute."

"He wants Peg too."

"Well, get her."

He goes to the stairs and yells. "Hey, Peg! Dad wants you!"

Belle's voice is angry behind him. Like she's speaking through gritted teeth.

"Brian, go *up* and get her. Do not scream in my house."

"Sorry," he says.

But he isn't sorry. He's pissed off. His sister gets to go down there while he doesn't. Why? Because he's got a prick, that's why. Well so does his fucking father. And what's the big deal anyway? He's already seen pretty much all there is to see of her. Except for her ass. And her cunt.

He didn't dare look that far when he was cleaning up in front of her. He knew his dad was watching. But thinking about what he *didn't* see is making him hard again. Funny how that takes the edge off his anger.

Peg's at the top of the stairs.

"What now?" she says.

She wants no part of any of this. She wants to wish it away. All of it. Maybe her entire life. But if it wasn't clear to her before it's crystal clear nowadays that wishing is like praying and you had to be blind or stupid or both to do either. So she follows her mother down the stairs.

Her father is fitting a black low-pressure nozzle into the spray wand. Thank god for that at least. She's used the pressure washer on her father's car and knows that even a medium-pressure nozzle has enough kick to it to bring down a low-flying bird. You don't play spray-me-with-the-garden-hose with that thing.

Her father looks up and smiles.

"There's my girls. All done, Belle?"

"Yes."

She holds the dress out for him to see.

"Great."

Her father produces a pocketknife and snaps open the blade and walks over to the woman chained against the wall. She can see the woman tense. She can feel herself tense. She can't for the world imagine herself in her position.

This is awful.

Her father cuts away the rag at her hips and the woman is naked.

Wholly naked for the first time and she glances at the thicket between her thighs but it's only a glance. It's her face that compels her. She does not see vulnerability in that face. She's not sure what she sees. Only that the woman is looking directly into *her eyes* now and Peg is amazed at herself because she's able to meet and hold that gaze which is at once predatory as a hunting bird's yet open as a child's.

The woman's nose twitches.

Her eyes move down Peg's body. To her belly.

To the mound of her belly invisible beneath the hoodie.

Impossibly, softly, she says, *"Bah-bee."*

Peg flinches.

There's the urge to just goddamn run. To just get the hell out of there. Yet she's aware that this is not an accusation, not a confrontation, nothing like that. This is not like Ms. Raton today. This is something else entirely. Did she mishear it or imagine it or was there pleasure in her voice? *Who and what* is *this woman?*

Nobody else seems to even have noticed. Her father's walking slowly around her, inspecting her. Her mother is watching her father.

She can read her mother's expression.

Not good.

The woman's eyes are still fixed on her belly.

She's almost grateful when her father holds out the woman's filthy rag to her.

"Take that out to the burn barrel," he says. "Torch it, then come on back."

"Yes," she says. "Okay, I will."

Cleek looks to his wife, who is frowning, her arms crossed over her chest, hugging the dress.

"You got something on your mind, Belle?"

"Do we really need Peg down here? She's sixteen."

"You think she doesn't get an eyeful in the girls' locker room?"

"That's different. Those are girls. This is a . . ."

"Woman. Yes, I know. I'm aware of that. Hey, Belle?"

"Yes?"

"Do me a favor and leave this to me, okay?"

He thinks, *always in my face. If it's not one thing it's a goddamn 'nother.*

He puts on the work gloves and checks the old rusty drain in the floor. It's clear. He picks up the spray wand. He turns on the pressure washer and pulls the trigger.

Cold soapy water blasts the woman in a sixty-five-degree arc all up and down her body. It buffets her flesh like a wind-whipped flag. He's never seen anything quite like it before except in those movies where some guy's being subjected to g-force acceleration. She's closed her eyes against it and closed her mouth against it and she's tossing her head side to side. When it hits her chafed bloody wrist she opens her mouth and screams.

He lets go of the trigger.

He turns to his wife and smiles. Or sort of half turns. Because he's sporting an erection you'd have to be dead to miss. He wasn't aware of it but Belle's stepped back nearly all the way to the stairs. She almost returns the smile, she takes a shot at it, but not quite.

"Let's see how we did," he says.

The woman is shaking her head and sputtering out the white film of water that slides down her body from head to toe. He has a look.

"Not bad," he says. "Need to get her back though. And then for some of this, need to get in closer."

Brian's throwing free throws when Peg walks back from the burn barrel. Darlin's trying to rebound for him. Which means chasing a ball she can barely get her arms around. Brian's tolerating this.

They all hear the woman scream and it stops them dead. Darlin's brow furrows like it does when she's puzzled. Peg's brother only smiles at her.

"I always miss out on the good stuff," he says.

"That's the *good* stuff? What the fuck is wrong with you, Brian? Jesus!"

She trudges back toward the cellar.

"Peg said a bad word," she hears her sister say behind her.

Which one? she thinks. *Fuck* or *jesus?*

In the cellar she's immediately aware of two things. First, her mother has moved so far away from this she's practically on the steps. She's clutching at the dress so hard her knuckles are white. Second, her father has moved in close, he's only a few feet away now and the water is pounding at the woman, her face pure agony as he moves the wand from her crotch to her thighs to her belly to each of her breasts and back down again, hurried strokes like he's painting some wall except that this wall is moving, writhing with each stroke of the wand that's got to be torture on her skin, the dressing from her side wounds sodden at her feet. She watches this and can practically feel it on her own skin like she's the woman and the woman's her and sees the woman's eyes go to the two of them standing back by the stairs and silently *plead* with them.

She's saying something. Or trying to say something *"Maithairs,"* she hears but that's all.

Her father varies his stroke. Up her breast and up her arm . . . to her wrist. *The wrist she reached for him with, the hand that grabbed him.* Her wrist black now with caked blood frothing white. The woman *howls,* absolutely *screeches.* Gasps. And then howls again and it's fucking huge. Peg has never heard a sound like this and never, ever wishes to hear it again.

"Daddy, please! Daddy! *Stop!* She's *hurt!* YOU'RE HURTING HER!"

She's never made quite so big a sound herself.

He releases the trigger, turns to her. She guesses she's surprised him. Well, she's surprised herself. And mom too. Mom's looking at her like, is this my daughter? My little Peggy? Who played so quietly as a child I had to check her in her playpen to make sure she was alive? Or so the story went.

"Please, dad. Please. Enough."

Her father looks . . . dazed or something. Like she's broken him out of some strange deep concentration. He shakes his head.

"She's not clean," he mutters and turns on the spray again.

Pummels her wrist again.

And there's that pig-being-slaughtered screech again.

"Fuck this!" Peg yells and turns for the stairs. Her mother tries to stop her but it's only halfhearted. Her mother's hands fall away almost as soon as they touch her. But her father's heard her too and he's turned off the spray.

"Get your ass back down her, Peg. Goddammit!"

And she's halfway up the stairs knowing her father's right behind her, that her mother won't try to hold him there either, won't dare to, when she hears something that stops them all.

From the woman. In a very small voice. A voice thick with tears.

"P-puhleese."

They're all turned to her then. Did she really say that? Peg thinks. Was that our language? *Please?* She's nodding to them. She says it again. The sound of it makes her heart race.

"P-uhleese."

Her father smiles and drops the pressure wand clattering to the wet cellar floor.

"Well, I'll be a son of a bitch," he says. "Belle? Peg? Go get some towels. And the first-aid kit. We'll need to patch her up again." He shakes his head. "I'll be a pure damn son of a bitch!"

Nineteen

The girl's actions have surprised her. She has begged them both for aid ("Will you help me, mothers?") but has not actually expected it. She is grateful. And very much wounded. Everything stings. Her entire body. She feels rubbed raw as if by sand. She's freezing. Her breasts ache. Her hair hangs wet in her eyes so that she can barely see and she has not yet the strength to shake it free.

The man steps closer. Licks some spittle off his lips.

The man is a dog with the foam of madness on his lips.

"Finally had enough, have you?" he says.

"Puh-leese."

She says it a third time. To him. Just him.

"I take well to manners," he tells her.

He goes to the winch and cranks it down. Lets some of that tension out of her arms—so that they're suspended at around shoulder length. He's giving her a gift. A little bit of comfort.

He can see that she appreciates it too, relief apparent on her face.

They're making friends here.

Belle walks down with the first-aid kit and towels. Peg's not with her. He decides to let Peggy skate on this one at least for the time being. No point making another scene down here. He'll have a talk with his damn daughter later.

"Dry her off," he says.

His wife hesitates.

"Her arms. You loosened her arms?"

"Don't worry."

"Says the man with nine fingers," she says.

Cleek can't help it, he bursts into laughter. The damn thing still throbs like a sonovabitch and he's been popping half Vicodins like they're antacids all day but Belle has actually made a *joke* and it's actually *funny!* The tension in the room bursts and drains away like all that dirty water on the floor. Belle smiles too. A real one this time.

He reaches into the back of his belt and pulls out the .45 and puts it to the woman's head.

"The doctor is in," he says.

"Dry as a bone, now. We don't want her coming down with something," Chris says.

The woman's shivering and Belle can hear those nasty teeth chattering but less so as she goes about her business, starting with her hair which is still matted, which will take a lot more washing and a hell of a stiff brush before it will be anywhere near decent but she's struck that it's such thick, healthy hair and wonders how that can be given the life she's led. Or that Belle supposes she's led.

She moves down to her face and neck, drying these quickly because gun or no gun and even with the towel between them she doesn't like the proximity to that goddamn mouth of hers. She dries each arm and as she does realizes that her husband's done his job quite well, if brutally. She's pretty clean. Not much grime coming off on the towel at all. But then comes the hard part.

Her torso. Her breasts and belly. Her privates.

She doesn't want to touch these. But Chris is expecting her to so she does and *as she does,* as she runs the towel over her breasts, a curious thing happens. There's a tingling where there shouldn't be. That's not possible, she thinks. That's ridiculous. So she runs the towel roughly over her belly and even more roughly over her ass and the fur between her legs—she thinks of it as fur, not pubic hair. But there it is again. That tingling.

She denies the feeling. She curses the feeling and curses this woman who by all rights shouldn't even be here, who should be out digging up roots and berries or lord knows what and truth be told, curses her husband too. She sweeps the towel down over both legs as quickly as possible.

"There," she says.

And stands away.

The female touching her reminds her of Second Stolen touching her. The wish to touch and yet not to touch, both at the same time, which she has read quite clearly. The Woman taught Second Stolen not to wish to touch her the hard way. With a thick branch of birch which she whipped across the girl's thighs until she lay huddled whimpering on the floor of the cave.

Second Stolen is gone now. They're all gone.

The Woman is alone with prey and monsters.

Cleek has applied bacitracin and clean dressings to both the wounds at her side, which are healing remarkably well, and her left ankle. Now he moves to her right ankle and slips the cuff up slightly so that he can get at the swollen red chafing there and swabs the antiseptic over it and wraps it tight.

He stands and sees that she's holding her hands out to him, palms up, so that he can get at her wrists. Almost a gesture of supplication he thinks. And perhaps it is. Her wrists are much worse. Particularly the right one—the one she worked free. The one she tried to throttle him with. It's not only bleeding, it's leaking a thin yellow pus.

He attends to the left one first. Cleans away the blood, swabs it, bandages it. Then he turns to Belle.

"Honey? Throw some alcohol onto one of those sterile pads, would you?"

The woman's had no problem with any of this so far. If anything she's seemed grateful. But that could be pure exhaustion. She's clearly exhausted. This next bit could go down a little bit harder. He should probably warn her. He takes the pad from Belle and holds it up for the woman to see.

"This is gonna hurt," he says and makes a face, pulls his lips back, a grimace of pain.

She looks at him questioningly. She doesn't get it.

"Owwwww!" he says and hisses and makes that face again.

She nods.

He applies the pad to the worst of the damage. Her fingers stiffen but she holds the wrist steady and doesn't make a sound. Good girl, he thinks.

"Soak me another, hon," he says. "Make that two."

When he's finished the room smells of alcohol. He lights a smoke and stands back to admire his work. Looks good—clean and fresh and good.

"Let's see that dress."

Belle holds up her project.

"It buttons up along the sides," she says. "So you don't have to untie her or anything."

"That's good. Try her on."

Belle's hesitant as ever around the woman but she walks over and lifts the dress. The woman shifts to one side as though trying to escape it. Like it's some living thing. Belle flinches.

"Go on. She's not going to do anything. All this is new to her, that's all."

He's not sure Belle believes him but she lifts the dress and pulls it down over the woman's head and drapes it across her body. He can see her hands are shaking as she fumbles with the buttons along one side and then the other. The woman's calm though. Just watching her.

"There," she says and steps away.

It's a very conservative baby blue dress, very Old World he thinks. Very rigid cuts. It looks incongruous as hell on her and that makes him smile.

"She looks like one of those polygamist types, doesn't she."

"Mennonite. The polygamists are Mormons."

"Right."

"You wanted it sturdy. That was the point."

"You did good, Belle. Very nice."

"Thank you."

He notices a funny thing. The woman was fine with being stark naked. Didn't seem to think a single thing about it. Now she looks sort of . . . well, he guesses the word is *shamefaced.* As though this little bit of domestication has left her absolutely humiliated. Again he has to smile.

"She cleans up pretty nice, doesn't she?"

"Should we feed her?"

"Yeah. We probably should. What've we got in the way of leftovers?"

"Stew. There's leftover stew."

"Fine."

When Belle's gone to heat the stew he goes to the sink and fills an old tin cup with water. The water's rusty but that's what you get down here. Better than nothing. He brings it over.

The woman looks down into the cup and immediately her mouth starts moving. She's thirsty as hell. He puts it to her lips and she sucks it down.

"You want more?"

This much she seems to understand. She nods vigorously.

He fills the cup again and she drinks. On an impulse he lifts his other hand into her long hair and is surprised as hell when she actually leans into it. Like she's savoring the contact.

Damn! This woman keeps surprising him.

***

Belle watches her husband feed the woman with the soup spoon. She's obviously starving, swallowing the stew without chewing, spilling some of it down over her chin. Her husband scoops it off her and feeds it back to her. Like she's a baby.

Belle has never had this kind of treatment from Christopher Cleek. Not even when she was running a temperature of one hundred four degrees down with the flu last spring. It rankles.

It rankles even more when he reaches up to stroke her hair.

She finishes the bowl. He wipes her chin with a sterile pad.

She's hiccuping.

No, wait. *She's crying.*

The bitch is actually crying. Tears rolling down her cheeks.

"Go raibh maith agat," she says.

"Thank you," Chris prompts her.

She doesn't understand. Belle thinks the whole thing's ridiculous. First dressing her up. Now trying to teach her to speak. Trying to teach her *anything.*

The woman's nothing but a savage.

"Thank you," he prompts again.

She still doesn't understand. Correction. An *ignorant* savage.

"Thaaank you," Chris drawls. "Thaaaank you."

"T-aank ooo," she says. *As if to belie me.*

It doesn't mean anything. A parrot could do as much. A mynah bird. She remembers seeing one on *The Tonight Show* who could imitate a duck or a monkey or even a cat.

Chris turns to her and smiles.

"See? She's learning," he says.

So is Belle. Learning more about her husband every minute of every day.

She's had time now to go into his study and have a look at his books. The picture isn't good. They owe money on nearly everything.

The second mortgage, the Escalade, the office. The interest on their credit cards is ridiculous. And now he's buying the Bluejacket properties. With what? Peg will be going off to college soon. Then Brian. They'll both want cars. He brings in good money from his practice and his investments are paying out good dividends but she wonders how he intends to juggle all this.

How he sleeps nights as well as he does.

And she wonders about this obsession of his.

This thing. This woman.

TWENTY

Genevieve sat at the end of Vance & Eddie's bar farthest from the door nursing her second Dewar's rocks of the evening and listening to Jerry Lee Lewis croon "I Only Want a Buddy Not a Sweetheart" and rattle that ol' piano against a Dixieland band while on the TV Giada De Laurentiis constructed some sort of pasta dish with a cream-of-sweet-potato sauce and broiled shrimp. Which looked quite tasty.

The bar was pretty dead tonight. A handful of local businessmen up front and only she and Ginger among the regulars. She didn't really get along with Ginger—a stringy ash blonde whose sole passions seemed to be clothes-and-shoe-shopping and local businessmen—the second of which passions she was indulging at the moment. Andrew, the bartender, she did get along with and was glad of the company when he walked over.

"Care for something to soak that up, Genevieve? Mussels are fine tonight."

"I'll just take some fries and mayo, thanks."

"One trip to Europe and you're eatin' like a frog?"

"Ribbet."

He called in the order.

"Your little charges giving you heartaches again? You're frowning, my dear. Bad form in a bar."

She hadn't been aware of it.

"They're not so bad."

"Boys still checking out that cute butt of yours?"

"I took a shot at dressing more or less like a nun. But nothing seems to work."

"You should be glad it doesn't. Keeps them interested."

"Right. But interested in what?"

"They have my complete and utter sympathy. I guarantee I wouldn't be able to tell a triangle from a square if I was a kid and you were bending over your daily lesson plan."

"Sweet, Andrew. You think if I told them which way I swing it would dampen things down a bit?"

"Honey, that'd only make it worse. What's with the paper?"

She hadn't been aware of fingering the note in front of her either.

"A phone number. Parents of one of my students. I'm pretty positive this girl is pregnant."

"Ouch. So you're telling the parents?"

"Shouldn't I?"

"That's a toughie, Genevieve. Could make things worse for her."

"You think so?"

"I'd say that nine times out of ten if they don't know already and some outsider *does* know she's gonna have hell to pay at the family hearth and home."

"But it's going to be very obvious very soon."

He shrugged. "Hey, it's your call. My dad always told me not to try and change a woman's mind once she's set on something. Think I'll heed the old man on this one."

Down the bar Ginger held up her empty wineglass and he moved away.

She sipped her scotch and considered.

She'd left her cell phone in her desk at school again. Maybe that was a sign.

And maybe not.

Andrew was right, she knew, to think this might be a mistake. It amounted to interfering. But she wished back then and still did that somebody had interfered with Dorothy, a gifted pianist and her first lover—their brief high school affair an experiment for both of them. Dorothy had gone off to college with a double major in music and psychology only to get herself pregnant by her music teacher, who then got scared of fucking a student and dumped her.

Dorothy was just then showing according to what she heard, when they found her naked, faceup on the floor of her dormitory bathroom.

Her wrists slashed the *right* way.

She heard the *ding* of the call bell behind her and knew that would be her french fries but by then she was already on the move toward the pay phone by the restrooms in back, paper in hand.

"Ah, hell," her father said. "Never fails at dinnertime. Peg, you want to go see who that is?"

She got up from her chair and walked down the hall to the phone and waited for the answering machine to kick in.

Hello, was what she heard. *This is Genevieve Raton and this message is for Mr. or Mrs. Cleek. Peggy is a student in my geometry cl—*

She cut off the message. Deleted it. Erased the number from caller ID.

Good god.

She walked back to the kitchen and sat down in front of her salad.

"Wrong number," she said.

Genevieve hung up the phone and wondered if she should try again. She'd heard the message on the machine—it was the father's voice. Somebody had heard hers too. Somebody had hung up on her.

She was still wondering when she returned to the bar and her french fries.

Andrew set a fresh Dewar's rocks in front of her.

"You're up to your buyback," he said.

"Thanks."

He leaned toward her and cocked his head.

"Well?"

"No answer."

He just looked at her for a moment, expressionless.

"I should let it lay, right?"

He shrugged.

"I should."

Below the phone number was the Cleek address, written in her neat loopy script. *No,* she thought. *Not a good idea.*

She crumpled up the scrap of paper in her fist. Andrew smiled. She pushed it away toward him across the bar.

Then she thought about Dorothy again. And something told her she should close no doors on this. Not yet.

So that when his back was turned to her she retrieved the ball of paper and slipped it into her purse.

PART THREE

TWENTY-ONE

Cleek could not have said later what got him out of bed that night and saw him padding down the stairs in his boxers and T-shirt and slippers. It could have been any number of things that woke him. A dog barking. A tree branch scraping the window in a gust of summer breeze. It could have been anything that kept him awake. Concern that she'd escaped somehow or hurt herself trying. The urge to see her once again in that Mennonite dress. To touch her wooly hair. Anything.

Belle knew what woke her. Cleek did. A creak on the stairs and an empty space beside her on the bed. She listened. Heard the front door open and close again. Felt her eyes pool with angry tears. The silence of the house deafening until filled with her own wracking sobs against the feather pillow.

Brian had never slept at all. So that when he heard his father's footsteps in the hall and then on the stairs and heard the sounds of his mother's muffled crying it took no leap of logic to determine that his father had not gone downstairs for a drink of water or a late-night snack but for other reasons entirely and when he heard him open and close the door his intuitions were confirmed. Lighter on his feet than his father—and quieter—he followed.

The two girls slept. Peg's sleep mercifully dreamless at the moment though that would change by morning as now it always did. Darlin's sleep filled with children. Children who liked her. Children who wanted to be kissed.

Twenty-two

Now that he's here he knows exactly *why* he's here. It's no mystery to him at all and shouldn't have been from the start. He flips on the light and sees that she's wide-awake and staring at him in that watchful cautious way of hers. He sees her in that dress. He loves that dress. Belle did a fine job there. *Damn* fine job. Mennonite, Mormon—what's the difference? They're all good to their menfolk right?

Respectful.

Not like some.

Some women, all they think about is *fi-nances*. Don't know the bold strokes. Worry that financial stuff like a dog worries a bone. Can't see the forest for the trees. Don't know the wheel from the deal.

He doesn't remember doing it—he's been stuck in his own mind here for a second or two he guesses—but he's practically on top of her now. Close enough to reach out and touch. She doesn't look all too worried about that. Could be she'd like to be touched. Seemed to like it this afternoon. That pat on the head.

But he's thinking that maybe it's not his hand she wants this time.

He's thinking it's cock. *Cock-co-cock-co-cock-co-cock. Cockadoodledoo. Anycock'lldo.*

Slut, he thinks.

You bit my fucking finger off.

Brian sees it all through his peephole. His father, the lawyer, upstanding citizen, Christopher fucking Cleek, PTA, Rotary and

Kiwanis, with his hand on the woman's collarbone, *stroking* her collarbone and then moving down to her breasts, the woman and his father standing eye to eye—though while her eyes are on his face his father is looking elsewhere, over toward the wall. Weird. It strikes him that his father's chickenshit. That he can't look her in the eyes. He hadn't expected that.

Then he's unbuttoning the side of her dress.

He's aware that his mouth has gone dry and is hanging open—he's mouth-breathing again, which he hasn't done since the second grade—and that he's clutching the wad of dirty gum so hard it's gone soft again.

His father pulls the dress up and drapes it over the woman's shoulder.

He can see everything now. Her bush. No—her *cunt.* Everything.

His father drops trou.

And something else hasn't gone soft on either of them.

It is the way of the world and she has expected this. There is a time to dominate and attack and a time to submit and this is just another submission in a series she has lately suffered at his hands. He now spits on one of those hands and strokes her cunt and spits again and strokes his cock, takes her ass in the other hand—she smiles to herself, the wounded hand and lifts her, enters her and begins to work. And it is work because she is dry inside, has been dry since the death of First Stolen, who filled her as this one never could, whose teeth marks remain on her shoulder to this day.

She thinks of First Stolen and his teeth and his cock and hands and thus makes it easier for the man, makes her cunt slicker. She does this as she focuses on the hole in the cellar door. A small hole but one she hasn't missed. Behind the small hole there is an eye which watches in the dark. In that eye she has recognized the same cruelty as in the man.

Only younger. And sweeter to the taste.
She nods to the eye and smiles.

Jesus! Brian flinches away from the peephole as though she'd poked him in the eye. She sees him! She knows he's there! How the hell can she know that? He hasn't made a sound.

And this is the second time she's caught him.

His cock retreats into his hand.

But then he thinks. Who cares what she knows? She can't tell anybody. *No speaka da English.* His eye returns to the peephole again. Fuck what she knows or doesn't know.

His father is grunting. He can hear him grunting which means it's loud. He's nearing home base. It occurs to him that he's watching his own dad down there. Is there something incestuous about that? Something *gay?* He doesn't think so. But he doesn't much care one way or another. He's watching this woman get fucked, that's all. He's watching her tits fall up and down, watching her thighs quiver with each of his father's thrusts. He can almost smell her sweat.

And then suddenly he's coming. He's shooting jizz all over the grass at the base of the cellar door. It's fucking *pumping* out of him in jets, in spurts. Like he's hemorrhaging out here and his cock is so sensitive he has to take his hand away or he's going to groan out loud or faint dead away but it's shooting out of him anyhow—his cock isn't done with him yet—and he's trembling all over and shooting and then finally he's still.

The man clutches at her breast as though he wants to rip it off her body and then moans and shudders and releases into her.
If she has a child by the man she will kill it.
She has done so before.

Cleek thinks that once this really got going it was probably the best damn fuck of his life.

Despite the odor of her mouth.

So what's wrong here? Why is it that he can't wait to tuck his dick back into his shorts? Is he afraid of disease? He isn't, not really. He can't see her having the AIDS virus living alone out there in the woods. And anything else is treatable as the common cold nowadays.

What, then?

He can't figure it.

He looks at her. At her face, her eyes. And there it is.

He sees something cold and blank and without any emotion whatsoever or any regard for him at all. He sees himself looking back at himself.

He feels something vaguely like shame.

He buttons her up. She looks fine. Like he's never been there at all. He turns off the cellar light and leaves her in the dark.

The Woman shifts a bit against the wooden plank behind her. When the man was fucking her pushing her back against it she had felt it give slightly, heard it give slightly. The man had not. The man was busy fucking her. She shifts her body up and then down with the plank wedged between one vertebra and the next and feels it give some more. It hurts.

But she will work on this.

TWENTY-THREE

At quarter past three in the morning Genevieve Raton rolled over out of her sleep and out of a dream in which she was burning autumn leaves in the fireplace on her dad's old farm long since sold in favor of a condo in Sarasota, realizing much too late that the flue wasn't working right, wasn't drawing correctly, and that leaves alight with flame were burning on the hardwood floor.

Awoke with her left forearm shoved right into Laura Hindle's face.

Laura grunted and opened her pretty green eyes.

"Sorry," she said.

Laura yawned and smiled. "What's with you tonight, kiddo? You're not ordinarily a thrasher."

"No, I'm not."

"This is the third time, you know."

"It is?"

"Yep. The first time you kneed me in the belly. The second time we went hip to hip. C'mere."

She opened her arms and Genevieve nestled in.

She felt comforted immediately. The flesh comforted. It always did. The flesh was warm and safe. By now they knew each other's bodies almost as well as they knew their own.

"Is it that preggy kid? The one who reminds you of Dorothy?"

"I don't know. I was back at my dad's house. So maybe. She used to visit me there all the time. My parents thought we were only friends."

"You were friends."

"You know what I mean."

Laura was a social worker by day and a part-time bartender at Vance & Eddie's by night. She knew how to draw you out. Sometimes all it took was a silence at just the right time. Like now.

"Old dead leaves," she said.

"Huh?"

"I was burning old dead leaves."

Laura pulled back a bit and regarded her. Then gently kissed her forehead.

"Maybe you still are."

"As in . . . ?"

"Yes. Fallen leaves. You really did love her, didn't you?"

"Not enough. Not enough to make her stay."

"Come on. You know better than that. People can't make other people stay. They only stay if they want to. Or need to."

Of course. She knew the truth in that. It had been a bitter truth at the time. But she was so very young then. And when you're young pain can take a long time to go away. And leave its residue forever.

She looked up into her lover's eyes.

"Do *you* need to? Stay, I mean?"

Laura kissed her again.

"I don't know what I'd do without you," she said. "I really don't."

Twenty-four

Peg awoke sweaty and disturbed. She didn't know by what. She almost never remembered her dreams, especially the bad ones. But she felt sure she'd had a bad one.

Her mother was standing in the doorway. Darleen was already out of bed and somebody was running water in the bathroom.

"What are you doing, Peg? Time for school."

"I'm not feeling so good, mom. I'm really not. Okay if I stay home today?"

Her mother looked angry. She didn't know why she would, first thing in the morning.

"There's nothing wrong with you," she said. "Get up."

"It's only a half day. Teachers' conferences, remember? Please? If I get up I'm gonna be sick."

It was true. She felt queasy.

If she got up there would be breakfast. The very thought of breakfast made her stomach turn. Her mother waved her hand in front of her face like she was swatting at a pesky fly.

"I don't have time for this. Fine!"

She stalked away.

What the hell was *that* about? she thought. She wasn't about to ask.

But she'd bet it had something to do with her dad.

Or that strange, almost fascinating creature in the cellar.

She pulled up the covers and closed her eyes and when the sounds of morning in the Cleek household eventually ceased, fell back to sleep.

***

Brian was standing at the school bus stop when the Escalade glided by. His father gave him the usual salute and Brian returned it.

With a lot more vigor than his dad was used to seeing.

Peg's desk was empty. With the kids all working on their pop quiz that was all she really had to focus on. *The desk was empty.* Up to today her attendance at least had been perfect even if her work was not. She thought, what now?

Laura was right. She was still burning leaves for Dorothy. In her arms she'd drifted off to sleep again and woke in the same position so evidently her thrashing had been over for the night. That didn't mean it was over for good though. In a way she'd been thrashing around all day today.

By the time the school bell rang a good quarter of the kids were still working on the quiz and a collective groan went up from those who hadn't finished. It hadn't been a particularly tough quiz. But then it wasn't a particularly bright class either.

"Enjoy your half day of freedom," she said. "Leave your papers on my desk, please."

She watched them file by and thought, they sure can vacate fast. A few smiled at her, a few said *bye,* but for the most part they were just in a hurry to get the hell out of there. That was fine with her. She'd have time for a smoke back by the ticket booth with Bill Fulmer before the conference.

She wondered what Bill would say about what she was thinking.

She dug the paper with the Cleeks' phone number and address on it out of her purse, placed it on her blotter and smoothed out all the wrinkles.

The bus ride home was typically manic when you had a bunch of kids with a half day off. Loud and obnoxious. Kids throwing spitballs in back. Guys flicking the earlobes of the girls in front of them. Some days he might have gotten a little obnoxious himself, what the hell. But today he had other things on his mind. Good things. Important things.

So that when Cyndi walked up the aisle and sat down beside him she was a distraction he didn't need.

"Hey, Brian. A bunch of us are going to the movies. The new *Twilight* movie. Want to come along?"

"Nah. *Twilight*'s lame. Besides, I gotta get home. Got stuff I gotta do."

Cyndi never had glommed on to the fact that he'd planted gum in her hairbrush. The poor kid really liked him. He could tell she was disappointed. But that's what she was—a kid. *Just a kid.* Pretty though. Too bad.

"Okay, then," she said. "Maybe next time."

"Sure. Next time."

Like there would ever be a next time.

He watched her slink back down the aisle to her seat and in a little while his stop came around and the door creaked open and he got off the bus.

Peg was lying on the couch, still in her pj's and covered by an old quilt, reading *Under the Dome* for the third time when he came rushing in headed straight for the kitchen. She considered saying something like *what's the big hurry, Brian?* but she knew it would come out bitchy because bitchy was how she was feeling and besides, they were just about to bust Barbie and Rusty out of jail and gruesome though it was, that was a part she liked.

So she said nothing. He didn't even notice she was there.

The note on the refrigerator beneath the magnetized ELVIS LIVES photo was in his mother's hand. *Darlin's dental appointment* it said, which he already knew. *Sandwich stuff in the fridge. Feed dogs, Brian. Home by three. Mom.* No X's and O's today. His mother had been in a mood.

Instead of making himself a sandwich he wolfed down what his sister called a little-man cookie and pocketed a couple more. Took the key ring off its hook on the support ring and went back outside. He noted the old rusty push mower which had probably belonged to his grandfather leaning against the porch, one of its broken blades lying beside it. It had been down in the cellar along with all that other junk the day they made room for *her.* He guessed his father had finally decided to throw something out.

He took the steps two at a time.

She glanced out the window and saw him loping toward the barn. She'd read the note on the fridge. He was supposed to feed the dogs. But she couldn't remember ever seeing him so eager to fulfill that particular duty.

She went back to the book.

In the barn the dogs were all excited barking and snapping but the dogs could wait. Till hell froze over as far as he was concerned. He had other stuff to do.

He went directly to his dad's old toolbox and rummaged inside.

TWENTY-FIVE

This is the boy whose eyes hunt her through the hole in the cellar door. The boy who burned her. The boy with the gun.

His body betrays him. He walks down the stairs and over to her as though it's nothing to him—but it is something. Something that makes him jitter inside. When he reaches out to her to do as his father has done, to remove her clothing, his hands tremble. The boy is a coward. It's time to show him that.

She hisses. Long and hard through her bared teeth. She is a cat, a snake.

She strikes him dead with her eyes.

Brian lurches back. And then thinks, *fuck you,* there's nothing you can do to me. His hands return to the buttons of her dress. By the time he's finished he's already got a hard-on. But he wants to play with her a while.

He takes a cookie out of his pocket. In the other pocket is the *real* toy. But for now he breaks the cookie in half and eats half of it and then holds the other half out to her. Daring her mouth. Daring those teeth.

She's fast, he knows. But he figures he's faster.

She won't accept it. She turns her fucking head away.

"What the hell's wrong with you?" he says. "I mean, who doesn't like cookies?"

So he eats that half too. He takes his time chewing, looking her over.

She's naked underneath there. All he has to do is lift the dress.

His hard-on's a whopper now.

He reaches into his other pocket and takes out his father's needle-nose pliers. He shows them to her. Snaps them open and closed a couple of times just to show her what they can do. He wonders if she gets the picture. He wonders if she bruises easily.

He pokes her in the ribs.

Pokes her again. Hard this time. The pliers aren't sharp enough to draw blood but you can bet they hurt. He pokes her in the belly. In each of her breasts. He hears the sharp intake of breath. Each time he pokes her she throws herself back against the shelf behind her but her nipples are hard now. He wonders if she's enjoying this.

He sure is.

Isn't that what happens to women when they're enjoying having sex? Their nipples get hard?

He throws her dress over her shoulder just as he's seen his dad do and stands there a moment to take her in. There's all of a sudden this really strange, really good sensation. And not just in his cock. He feels good all over, tingly, strong. If this is what power feels like, he likes it very much.

He runs his hands over her belly up to her breasts and squeezes. Her skin isn't as soft as he'd imagined but her nipples are huge and long as budding twigs. The woman squirms beneath his touch as though something dirty's touching her and he doesn't like that at all, there's nothing dirty about him, this is only natural. He's a guy and she's a woman and this is what women are all about, right? So fuck her. He grabs the tits again and squeezes so hard he thinks they'll pop.

She *growls* at him and sniffs the air and spits out some words in that stupid language he doesn't understand.

"Feoil ur! Muiceoil!"

"Fresh meat! Pig meat!"
She says this with contempt and presses back against the wooden

board behind her, feels it shift and give again, give a little more each time. The boy is confident now. The boy thinks he has power. If she can break this board he will not feel so confident anymore, not at all.

She can suffer his hands. The hands are nothing.

She repeats her words and Brian doesn't like that one bit. He gets her goddamn tone if not the meaning of the words. It's as though she thinks he's beneath her. As though she's somebody. *Time to show her who's who, Brian,* he thinks. Time to seriously fuck with her.

His parents haven't got a clue god knows but he's seen stuff like this on the Internet, exciting stuff that seemed like it was made just for him, just for Brian Cleek. There are dozens of sites—probably hundreds. They all make noises about *consenting adults* and *role play* and *submission* but he knows what they're really all about. They're all about *this.*

He reaches over with the pliers open this time and snatches up her left nipple in its serrated jaws and twists.

The woman jerks up and back but makes no sound. No hisses and no cursing—he assumes that was cursing—she just sucks it up. So he twists again. A full one hundred eighty degrees this time. Still no sound. *Let's see if she can go all three sixty* he thinks and jams his free hand into his pants working her and working himself and he's just about to come, he's *that close* when he hears footsteps pounding on the stairs behind him.

"Brian! What the hell are you doing?"

It's his sister Peg, closing in on him like a storm cloud. He palms the pliers and takes his hand out of his pants and suddenly he's scared. He's not in charge anymore. Far from it. Caught is what he is.

"You're in trouble now, you little shit."

"You got no need to be down here, Peg. This is guys' business. Men's business."

He's trying for indignation, for defiance. But he can see she's not buying any.

"Men's . . . ??? I don't see any men around here, you fucking little pervert!"

And that pisses him off. Really pisses him off. He's no pervert. He's doing what any guy would do under the circumstances. And what plenty of people do on the Net every day. Just who the hell does Big Sister think she is, anyway? His conscience? He doesn't need any.

"Screw you, Peg!"

He takes a step toward her and it's as though that single step has created some sort of force field between them because she takes one step back. He does it again and so does she and he realizes she's seen something in his face, he doesn't know what exactly but it scares her, she's a lot more scared now than he is. He's smiling. He considers the pliers in his hand. He considers his sister.

But no. There's his mom. There's his dad. This really is trouble and he might just be making it worse right now. He backs off and the force field disappears like an errant gust of wind.

"Get out of here, Brian," she says. "Our mother is going to hear about this. Your *father* is going to hear about this. Get out of here *now!*"

There's no choice but to give in. His sister's got her balls back. But he can't resist knocking into her shoulder as he passes.

"Good, Brian," she says. "I'll tell them about that too."

He's already thinking how to explain this—if there's any *way* to explain this—as he pounds his way up the stairs.

The girl is hesitant, frozen in front of her. Confused? Frightened? She can read tension but no further than that. She has shouted her brother away. That took courage. Her brother is a coward but he is also dangerous.

Slowly the girl steps toward her and pulls the clothing down off her shoulder to cover her body. It brushes the wounded nipple as it falls.

Peg works at the buttons. Surprisingly her hands are very nimble at this. Surprisingly she's not afraid at all.

"I'm sorry," she says. "About all of this."
The woman gazes down into her eyes.
"Go raibt maith agat, mathair," she says.

"Thank you, mother."

TWENTY-SIX

He was the product of what his father had taught him to be, who in turn was the product of what *his* father had taught him to be and she wondered how far back in sheer misogyny and greed the Cleeks actually went. She had married blind into this, impressed by his self-possession as a teenager, even more impressed by him in bed—or in fact for the first year or so, in the backseat of his father's Caddy. Her first and only lover.

Now, waiting for him at the kitchen table with her children assembled—Peg beside her and Brian and Darleen across from them—she felt like his broodmare more than his wife. Certainly not his lover. She couldn't even call herself his friend. These children were the issue of her life. Her only issue. She didn't count the other. She wouldn't count the other. These three only. She had nothing else in the world but them.

And of these only Darleen so far had escaped his . . . pollution. She had to call it that. That was what it was. Something *wrong* dumped into the stream. And you couldn't even be sure about Darleen, could you? She was far too young.

On Darleen the jury was still out.

It wasn't out on Brian.

Darlin' thought, momma's angry. Momma's *really* angry. Bri's done something to make her angry. And Peggy is too—she's angry. At him. She wondered what it was. It might be important to know what it was so that she wouldn't do the same thing sometime and make them angry at her too.

It was strange just sitting there, not talking, waiting for daddy.

She wanted to give them all kisses to make it all better.

She almost wanted to cry. But she wouldn't.

It was so strange. She didn't even want a cookie.

You're all alike, Peg thought. Men. You do what you want and to hell with the consequences. To hell with what the woman thinks, what the woman feels. It's all about you.

It was rumored around school that Ms. Raton was a lesbo.

She wouldn't blame her. Not one bit.

Brian felt like he had one chance and one chance only. A single card to play and that was it. He had seen his dad fucking her. He knew what nobody else did. If it came down hard on him, could he play that card? Would he dare to? Would it turn out better or worse for him if he did?

He didn't know. Hoped he wouldn't have to find out.

She heard the Escalade pull up outside.

"Darlin'?" she said. "Go to your room."

Her daughter was upset. And probably quite confused. Rightly so.

"Why? I didn't . . ."

"Don't worry, honey. This isn't about you. This is about your brother. Now go up to your room like a good girl."

She watched her slide off the chair and sulk her way out of the kitchen. She knew her daughter. Upset and confused she might be, but with Darleen it was always important to be *in on* things, not to be left out. That inquisitive spirit might be useful to her in the future or it might get her into very deep trouble. It was impossible to know.

She glanced at Brian, fidgeting in his chair with his hands folded in his lap as though he were in church faced with a long boring sermon. Then at Peggy glaring at him. Almost inexplicably she found herself furious at both of them. Him for what he'd done, obviously. But why Peggy? Why her?

For dragging me into this, she thought. That's why.

For seeing. And then reporting what she'd seen.

Female trouble he thought as he walked into the kitchen.

We got girl trouble here.

It had been a good day for him. Got a fine settlement from Air Canada for Steve Bachman's neck injury and filed those divorce papers for Ed Seymour, who was going to take his rich wife to hell and back for screwing their gardener, one Windy Brewer. What the hell kind of a name was Windy, anyway? And who would want to fuck him? It had been a real good day but it looked to him as though that was going to stop right here.

When Belle stood up at the table shaking with anger and pointing at him that about confirmed it.

"Do you want to know what your son did? Do you want to *know?*"

"Not sure I do," he said. "Goddammit, Belle. What the hell's going on? Where's the Toyota?"

"In the shop. Some idiot rammed into my driver's-side door at the IGA. Vicki Silverman drove me home. But never mind the damn Toyota, Chris. I'm talking about your son here! Your son! He didn't think anyone was home so he went down there. With her. Had her dress off. Had her *naked.* And he was touching her. And he was touching himself! If Peg hadn't caught him at it god knows what would have gone on in that cellar!"

He looked at Brian, staring down at the table like there was something really quite interesting crawling around on its surface.

"That true, son?"

Belle didn't even give him a chance to say yes or no.

"Peg *caught* him at it. Didn't you hear me? Why the hell are you asking him, is it true?"

"Calm down, Belle. He's just a boy."

"Just a . . . *calm down?* I will not calm down! He had one hand on her, and the other hand shoved down into his goddamn jeans, Chris!"

"I'm telling you to take it easy. Look at me, boy. Look at me when I talk to you."

His son didn't want to but he did. Chris smiled at him. Couldn't help it. Hell, the kid was a chip off the old block. In a way he was even proud of him. He was learning to be a man.

"Ah well, hey," he said, "no one's really hurt here, right?"

"No one . . . no one's . . . *what?*"

"He's a kid, Belle. An adolescent. Adolescents have urges. Boys will be boys, right? And all cleaned up like she is, I gotta say, she's not half-bad to look at, y'know? These things happen."

He had seen his wife mad before, but—in the parlance of his own adolescence—he had never seen her *flip out* before. And he had to wonder if it didn't have something to do with last night. Whatever it was, she got right up into his face with it.

"You can't fucking *do* this anymore!" she said.

Belle? Use the word *fucking?*

"You can't do this to us, Chris! This has gone too far! Have you lost your mind? You can't just stand there and smile when your own son thinks it's okay to . . ."

"Okay to what, Belle?"

"You're an officer of the court! She's a *human being!* Do you know what would happen to *all* of us if you got caught? Even what's going on with the goddamn dogs out there would be enough to put you in prison!"

"Anophthalmia, Belle. Your *shame.* Anophthalmia, remember?"

"I remember, all right. And I never condoned what you did. Never. But you can't just keep putting one thing on top of another and expect to get away with it forever! You can't! Enough's enough! I've had it!"

At this point so had he. His face burned.

"So what are you going to do, Belle. Huh? Tell me. What the fuck are you going to do about it?"

Her face had turned into one big ugly sneer. One big ugly sneer *at him.*

And he realized something. His wife had just this moment made a decision. It was like *inspiration* was all of a sudden written all over her. Her body went utterly rigid.

'I'm leaving, *that's* what I'm going to do about it!" she said. "And I'm taking the girls with me. You can have your little rapist son all to yourself. You're already teaching him every goddamn thing he needs to know, aren't you? You two can damn well burn in hell together, the two of you. But you're not going to hurt these girls anymore. It's finished. It's over. You hear me? Right now. You can't do this! *I* can't do . . ."

There was a moment when all he saw was a bright blank yellow. Like he was looking directly into the flash of a camera. And then he was hitting her in the stomach *one two three* with his whole body behind it, a sound like the heavy bag made when he still worked out on it back in the day and the next thing he knew his right fist connected with her left temple and he watched her go down, legs falling out from under her like a well-shot deer.

I can't? He heard himself roaring at her inert body sprawled across the linoleum. *I CAN'T?*

His kids were looking at him. Peg with horror. Brian with . . . what?

His son he couldn't read. Fuck it.

Then Peg was down on the floor beside her slapping her cheek.

"Mom? Mother?"

He brushed her away.

"She's okay. She'll be okay," he said.

He bent down and lifted her, his forearms under and through her armpits which were damp with sweat, an unpleasant feeling. And there was a taste in his mouth he didn't like. He wanted to spit. He kicked a chair out from the table next to Brian and sat her down. Positioned her carefully so she wouldn't fall out of it and gently held her there.

"Get a cold cloth, will you, Peg?"

His daughter didn't move. His daughter just stood there, frozen, angry-looking.

"Peg!"

He watched her snap out of it finally, get out from under wherever the hell she was and walk over to the sink, wet a cloth and kneel beside her mother.

And that was when the doorbell rang.

TWENTY-SEVEN

"Want to get that first," her father said. "See who it is?"

He'd flipped a switch and was all at ease now. That quiet almost Southern drawl of his.

Her father was fucking crazy.

She felt a deep conflict here. On the one hand to go to the door would be to admit into their home the potential for some sort of normalcy, a breath of air from the outside world, some person or persons who in all probability *weren't* beating up on their wives and keeping women in the fruit cellar and their kids under lock and key. On the other hand there was the potential for all this shit to be exposed. The potential for shame. Eventually for ridicule.

But Peg was seething. Furious not only with her father but with her mother too. She'd sat there stunned during her mother's tirade, not believing what she was hearing. *Enough's enough?* Finally? Now? She's leaving him *now?* Just because Brian's shown himself to be the sick little fuck he is? When what's been going on out in the barn has been going on for years? Why wasn't it going *too far* when he nightly raped and finally knocked up his own fucking daughter? Why wasn't enough *enough* then?

You're taking me with you? Over my dead body.

Screw her mother too. Darleen excepted, they could all go to hell.

She went to the door, opened it but then damn near closed it again. She was furious all right. But she wasn't quite prepared for this much.

"Ms. Raton?"

***

The look on Peg's face told her all she needed to know. That she was right. She saw fear and confusion and plenty of it. Even anger. She pitied the girl—she truly did—but this needed to be done. Her parents needed to know, if they didn't already. And if they did know, Genevieve was certain she could help.

She managed a smile.

"Hi, Peg. Going to let me in?"

"This . . . this really isn't the time . . ."

"Sure it is. Come on, Peg, I'm not going to hurt you. I'm here to help."

"You can't help, Ms. Raton."

"How do you know that?"

"I just . . . do."

This wasn't going well. She couldn't very well force her way in.

"You'd be surprised," she said. "I know counselors, doctors, all kinds of people."

"I said this isn't the *time*, Ms. Raton!"

She was thinking, *family spat?* Maybe the girl was right. Maybe this wasn't the time. But she was here now. She couldn't see herself leaving and then coming back if and when it was more convenient. But she was stumped for a good answer.

Then the father stepped out from behind her—Christopher Cleek—looking genial enough and smiling.

"Where's your manners, Peggy?" he said. "Please, come on in."

She stepped inside and he offered her his hand. The hand felt slightly clammy though the grip was firm. There was a scent coming off him though. Some kind of chemical smell. Like old booze—but it wasn't that. She couldn't place it.

He steered her into the living room.

"How are you, Ms. Raton? Geometry, right? I remember you from parents' night. Good to see you again. Please, have a seat. Can I get you anything? Cup of coffee? Soft drink?"

He directed her to the plush velvet chair. She sat facing the two of them on the couch.

"I'm fine, thanks," she said.

She wasn't fine. Not exactly. But it wasn't anything a cup of coffee was going to fix either. She'd never done anything remotely like this before—gone to the parents' house on some student's behalf. She was confident in the classroom. Here she felt shy, out of place and just a little scared. But mostly what she felt was determination. To get this out into the open finally. It was what somebody—anybody—should have done for Dorothy.

"May I talk to you and your wife privately, Mr. Cleek?"

"Call me Chris, Ms. Raton, please. And you are?"

"Genevieve."

"Genevieve. Beautiful name. You're French-Canadian?"

She smiled. "My dad was Louisiana Cajun, Mr. . . . Chris. He fell in love with a girl from Ottawa."

"He followed his heart."

"Yes, he did."

"That's good. We should all do that. She's not feeling too well, Genevieve. My wife I mean. She's having herself a nap. This is about Peg, I gather?"

"Yes."

"Then she should hear it, don't you think? My boy too. No secrets in this family. Brian? Come on in, son."

She'd seen him leaning halfway in and halfway out of the room against the door frame. *Lurking* was the word that came to her. A tall thin boy she vaguely remembered seeing around school but had never met.

Time to gird your loins, woman, she thought. Time to get on with it.

"I've observed some . . . distressing behavior lately, Mr. Cleek."

"Chris."

"Chris. Peggy's not looking well. She's had to rush off to use the ladies' restroom several times during class. Her studies are off. And she's taken to wearing clothes much too big for her."

He shrugged and smiled again, the picture of amiable old dad. "She likes to borrow my sweats. So?"

"Does Peggy have a boyfriend, do you know?"

She saw Peg's head dip down to her chest as though waiting for the ax. She hated doing this to the poor girl. But she was doing it *for* the poor girl.

"No," Cleek said. "And I'd know it if she did. Why?"

"I believe . . . I believe that Peg is pregnant, Mr. Cleek."

"Pregnant."

It came out flat, emotionless. She'd have expected much more. She'd have expected *something.*

"I am not!" Peg said.

And that was *not* emotionless. It was tense as hell and there were tears beginning to form behind the words. But Cleek seemed to ignore his daughter. Cleek's focus was directly on her.

"What makes you think my daughter is pregnant, Ms. Raton?"

She noted that they were no longer Chris and Genevieve, they were back on formal terms. It was actually a relief.

"She's *showing,* Mr. Cleek. Not very much yet but that won't last much longer."

"Any of your colleagues concur with this opinion, Ms. Raton?"

"What? I wouldn't know. I haven't discussed it with them. I thought it best to come directly to you and your wife."

"And you did well to do so."

He leaned in close and she knew what that smell was now. He smelled like old rotting meat. There were girls in class whose personal hygiene was well south of what it should have been and when they got their period they smelled the same way. Old spoiled meat.

And a meanness had crept into his voice that she didn't like.

"I thought you teachers were supposed to listen," he said. "You don't listen too well, Ms. Raton. I told you that Peggy didn't have a boyfriend and that I'd know it if she did, right? Didn't I?"

"Yes, but . . ."

"You accusing Brian here?"

He motioned toward his son. The boy was grinning. *What's going on here?* she thought. *What have I stepped into?*

"He's just a boy, Ms. Raton."

"No, of course not . . ."

"Dad," Peg was tugging on his arm. He pulled away.

"You accusing *me?*"

"No, I . . ."

Get out of here, she thought. There's something seriously wrong with this guy. She stood up. So did he.

"You saying that? *Are you?*"

She held her ground. Short of sprinting for the door there was nothing else she could do. Besides, this guy was beginning to piss her off too.

"I said nothing of the sort, Mr. Cleek."

"In my own home. You accuse me."

He was right in her face now—way into her space—and his voice had gone eerily soft.

"Right here in my own home," he said.

"I did not. I never said . . ."

But I didn't have to, did I? she thought. *You said it for me. You fucked your own daughter, you bastard, you sick piece of shit. You fucked her and got her pregnant and now I've stuck it to you, haven't I? You miserable sack of . . .*

She never saw it coming.

But Peg did.

Peg saw her father strike a woman for the second time that night.

Openhanded this time but with no less power and right across the side of her head. So that one moment Ms. Raton was standing there in front of her and the next she was on the floor, her head striking the antique pie safe so hard it rattled the plates inside. She saw her teacher's eyelids flutter once and then close.

"Jesus, daddy! What did you . . . ?"

"Shut up, Peggy. This is all your own damn fault, you little bitch. Get out of here! Go out to the barn. Go get me some rope!"

"Rope? What are you going to do with rope?"

"Go! Now!"

"No!"

"I'll go," said her brother.

She heard the front door slam. Her father was glaring at her. Her father wanted to hit her too.

"Get out of my sight," he said. "You brought this on. You and that sweet little cunt of yours. Go help your mother."

Twenty-eight

Darlin' hid.

Darlin'—*Darleen,* her name was *Darleen*—was hiding. She hid behind her sister's bed because her sister's bed was safe and heard loud voices and things going *thump* and she could feel bees buzzing up through the floorboards, she could feel bears coming out from the dark of the woods, there were black crows at the windows wanting to get in.

What she could do was ball herself up tight and kiss her knees. She could blink a hundred times and count them one by one.

That way she wouldn't cry.

She would count her blinks and kisses and wouldn't cry.

TWENTY-NINE

Genevieve Raton awoke at the end of a rope tied to her wrists. Being hauled across the yard on her belly by a madman.

She saw floodlights above a barn with its doors open. She felt hard earth and wet patchy grass. Heard dogs barking. Her arms felt like they were tearing out of her shoulder sockets. She saw the boy walking along beside her, grinning.

She turned on her hip to try to get to her feet but he was pulling her along too fast and she fell back down again, landed chin first. She tasted blood. Felt a hot pain score the inside of her cheek.

"Cleek!"

She was spitting blood at him. He didn't even turn to look. Just kept dragging her. She tumbled side to side, scraping herself hip to hip.

"Cleek!"

She saw Peg run to him from somewhere behind her, Peggy pulling at his arm, trying to stop him.

"Daddy! Stop, please! You can't do this! She's my *teacher*, daddy. She's my . . ."

"Friend? That what you were going to say? Your *friend* comes here to expose you for the little whore you are?"

She managed to get over on her ass, dug in with her feet like some rodeo cowboy and jerked at the rope. For a moment he lost his balance. Then he jerked back and she was on her belly again.

They were nearly to the barn.

"Daddy, you can't . . ."

He grabbed his daughter's arm and flung her to the ground.

o=

ed the rope the last few feet and lashed his end to the barn's door handle. Then he walked over to Peg, stunned, cowering beneath him in the dirt.

"Daddy, you can't," he said. "You can't. You can't! I have fucking *had it* with *you can't* and the women in this family! Your mother, your idiot sisters, you!"

Genevieve got up on one knee. Then to her feet.

"Please," she said. "Just let me go. I won't tell anyone about this, I promise."

Her voice sounded hoarse and distant to her.

Behind her Brian rapped her in the head with a stick. She hadn't seen the stick. It fucking hurt.

"Shut up, lady," he said.

"No, make that *all* women," said Cleek. He was on a tear now. "I have had it with all you goddamn bitches. You're leeches, every one of you! You suck a man dry. A man works like a dog every day and you suck him dry!"

He reached down and grabbed the neck of Peg's sweatshirt and yanked her to her feet. Then he had the shirt in both hands, shaking her. Peg was flailing at him.

She was not about to watch him beating up on his own daughter.

"Stop this!" she said. "Stop this right now!" And this time her voice was clear.

Brian rapped her in the ear. She almost went down again but managed only to stumble. She turned to go after him but he danced away laughing.

"You little fucker!"

She felt blood trickle down her neck to her collar.

Peg screamed. Cleek had his hand up under her sweatshirt clutching at her breast. Peg was trying to pull his hand away. He only clutched harder.

"Cleek! Damn you, Cleek!"

She turned to see if Brian was planning on whacking her again. He just smiled. The little snake.

"Cleek!"

He paid her no attention. *He was focused on his daughter's breast.*

"You know what you're good for, Peg?" he said. "You ridiculous whining bitches are good for one thing and one thing only and half the time you're miserable at that. You think I don't know who you are? You think I don't? You're no better than that thing in there. That thing in the cellar. That's where *all* of you belong. Every last cunting one of you!"

She had time to think, *what thing in the cellar?* and then he threw Peg down again—she was all knees and elbows, hitting hard—and started pulling on the rope, hauling her toward the open barn doors. She tried pulling back but it was useless. He was much too strong and much too furious. She could hear the dogs inside in a frenzy now. Something was happening out here and the dogs wanted in on it.

"Come on, Brian," he said. "This one we handle right away."

THIRTY

Her father's words dripped poison in her ears. *That's where* all *of you belong. Every last cunting one of you.*

She hung up the phone. The police said they were on their way. They were out in the middle of nowhere though. It would take them half an hour to get from town to her house if she was lucky. Her breast throbbed. Her ears rang.

Every last cunting one of you.

Am I next, daddy? Am I?

Momma? Me? Darlin'? In what order?

She was crying, sobbing.

The dogs were barking like crazy. She couldn't imagine what was going on out there or maybe she *could* imagine and didn't want to.

"No more," she said. "This has got to stop. Not any more . . ."

She took the keys off the support beam and ran past her mother's prone body to the hallway and out the back door.

Belle awoke to what she thought was probably at least one broken rib and the sight of her daughter's legs flashing by. She tried to speak but couldn't. She tried to sit but all she could immediately do was to get up on one elbow and try to breathe and ease the dizzy feeling. Everything hurt. Her head and ribs most of all—but everything.

She tried again. This time she was able to straighten her arm. There was a damp washcloth on the floor beside her and she used it on her face against the dizziness. It helped.

"Momma? I counted to a hundred. I didn't know what to do after that. Where is everybody? What's happening to the doggies?"

Darlin' stood hunched in the doorway, eyes wide, clearly scared. But she was right. The dogs were going nuts outside.

She didn't want her little girl to see her like this and it was painful as hell but she managed to sit and then slowly, to stand.

"Come here," she said. "Come here, hon."

Darlin' rushed to her and flung her arms around her waist.

Her ribs screamed.

"Easy," she said. "Please, honey. Go easy."

Brian slammed the double doors.

His father dragged *Rat-on* to the dog cage and tied her off to a link. The dogs were just on the other side, gnashing, frothing, barking up a storm, lunging at her through the wire fencing. Rat-on kept going *no no no* trying to keep her distance and at the same time loosen the knot at her wrists. But his father knew his knots.

"Hose!" his father said. "Nozzle it down, son. I want 'em *mean.*"

Had he fed the dogs today? Unh-unh. No, he hadn't.

So they would already be mean.

But he cranked the water and twisted the nozzle down to a single heavy stream which he sprayed half on George, Lily and Agnes and half on Rat-on. She kept trying to protect her face. He drenched her.

The cold water made her nipples hard.

Nice.

"Get 'em back," his father said.

So he concentrated on the dogs. Mama Agnes retreated to the doghouse. Growling, snarling at them. Fuck Mama Agnes. Lily and George fled to the back of the cage.

"You keep those two back there."

"Please," Rat-on said. "Stop this. I swear I won't say anything. None of this ever happened, okay?"

She was pleading. He liked that.

His father didn't seem to give a shit one way or the other. He simply untied the rope from the link, opened the cage door and dragged her short-leashed to the doghouse and pushed her down in front of it. Agnes snarled. Not at Rat-on but at his father. So his father did what he always did. Snarled right back at her and made as though to give the dog the back of his hand. Which she had felt plenty of times ever since she was a pup. She backed off, barking.

His dad threw the cage door shut.

Genevieve watched the dog. Watched the dog watching her. The look in its eyes scared the hell out of her. The look was practically feral, as though the dog were a wolf in the wild and not some domesticated animal in a cage.

On the other side of the cage the boy still had his hose on the other two. But not on this one.

This one was stalking her. Slowly closing in.

She knew she could not take her eyes off the dog for a moment. If she did it was going to attack. But what she could do was to try to inch crabwise away, get her back against the doghouse—maybe even get *inside* the doghouse where she'd be protected on three sides at least. And from there she could maybe kick the damn thing until it went away.

So that was what she did.

Oh, bad choice she heard Cleek say. *Can you say anophthalmia?*

But by then it was too late.

Thirty-one

The Woman is with them, out there with the dogs. She hears their animal spirit, something in them yet untamed. It soothes her, this wildness. It reminds her that tooth and claw is the nature of the world and the nature of each beast in it. That nothing in the wild dies without great loss and gain. That no kind of beast was ever meant to live in cages. Or damp dark places such as this one.

She hears keys at the door and a moment later it opens.

The girl rapidly descends. Turns on the light. Then pauses breathless to look at her.

Behind her she can hear the dogs' violent voices more clearly now. On the girl she smells fear. Fear and something else. Anger perhaps. Yes. And protectiveness. The girl is protecting someone. Perhaps the baby inside her.

Protecting the baby from her? She poses no threat. Not as she is.

But then the girl does the most astonishing thing. The Woman could never have expected it.

She steps over to her, gazes once into her face and then bends down and begins unscrewing the restraint on her left ankle.

Thirty-two

The child had been alive for nearly ten years but knew nothing of time. She was female but knew nothing of that either.

The child knew only the doghouse and the occasional venture outside to steal food from the others who were not hairless like her—she had huddled with them against the cold, slept with them curled around her, listened to their breathing which was not like her own—or to void herself or exercise her limbs.

For the child the world was always dark. Several shades of dark but always so.

She could smell herself. She could smell the others. So that she knew she was different from them but in what way she couldn't tell exactly except that she was hairless and they were not and they seemed to have no ability to grasp at things and hold them the way she did. Her teeth were long but theirs were longer. The pads on their feet were tougher. They were long and lean and she was thick and squat.

These things aside, they were family.

So that when she heard their rage and outrage it became hers too—and she braced herself against the wood behind her and waited for the shapes and shades of darkness to change from dark to darker. Which meant movement. Intrusion.

Perhaps the hand that stung.

She heard a low growl behind her and realized her mistake, that there were not three dogs in here but four, yet there was no time nor any way for her to fix that because the dog outside was inching closer and closer, Genevieve hoping against hope that a growl was all she was in for and when the thing inside the doghouse leaped out at her roaring—the thing that had no eyes but only empty eye sockets, its skin like dirty melted pink wax, *human, yes, but built like some kind of pit bull*—when the child-thing sunk its teeth into the flesh between her neck and shoulder and its yellow cracked claws into her arms all she could do was to reach back with her roped hands and try to pull it off her and scream and scream.

"Brian! Hose Agnes!" his father was shouting and so he did, Brian having a fine old time here, catching the dog full in the face, backing her off and listening to Rat-on scream.

"Okay, sis," he yelled, "let's see what you got!"

Inside the house Belle heard the screaming and so did her daughter and Darleen wouldn't let go of her, she was holding on for dear life and Belle's ribs were doing their own screaming. Finally she pushed her away and held her at arm's length.

"Darlin'? Baby? I want you to go back to your room right now. Lock the door and don't come out. Don't come out unless it's momma or Peggy, okay?"

She was squirming in Belle's grip, tears running down her face.

"Noooo . . . I want to stay *here* . . . with *you* . . ."

"You can't, honey. Now do as I say. It's really, really important. Okay?"

She let go of her and turned her around and gave her a little push. Darlin' ran for the stairs.

Then she turned too to find out just what the fuck was going on.

The child-thing was tearing at her, ripping at her back with its fingernails, tearing through her clothing to the naked flesh beneath and she heard herself mindlessly saying *get away get away get away* and pushing at it and whipping around so that finally she landed on top of it, heard the *whoosh* of air out of its lungs and smelled its awful breath full in her face but it let go of her and for a moment she was free.

She turned and scuttled back until she hit the chain-link cage and realized that all that flailing had done one good thing at least, she had some play in the rope that bound her—her left wrist was coming free. She tugged on it, clawed at it. She tried to stand but there seemed to be no strength in her legs. The child-thing was slinking toward her just as the dog had done. It was growling. Then barking at her. Some shrill approximation of a bark anyway.

You're not a dog, she thought, *you're human.*

And somehow it was all the worse for that.

She tried to stand again and fell and pulled at the rope. Her face was wet. She realized she was crying and that was when the child-thing leaped forward and sunk its teeth into her ankle. She felt bones break inside and shrieked and lurched forward, felt adrenaline rush through her like a hot burning liquor and suddenly her left hand was free of the rope and she slashed at the thing and clawed where its eye should be—the empty socket—and the child screamed a child's shocked scream and its hands went to its face. Then it shook its head like a wet dog and leaped again, blood and spittle flying.

It clawed down the length of her belly and *gripped* there deep. And no dog could do that. No dog could reach into her and grip there and haul itself the length of her while its other hand clawed into her breast to pull itself up farther and the last thing she heard before its teeth found her neck was the father saying *turn it off, son* and knew that to be endgame—the end of Genevieve Raton and the last thing she thought was—*Dorothy.*

Brian turned the water off and looked at his father. His father simply stood there, arms at his sides, expressionless.

Then he watched the dogs go at her.

Thirty-three

The Woman hears it all. The screams, the voices of the dogs, the voice that is like a dog's but is not a dog's and which briefly puzzles her. But what puzzles her most is this girl who has freed her legs and then her left wrist. Who touches her gently and yet is very afraid.

The girl reaches up to the Woman's right wrist and then draws back her hands. Her hands are trembling. The girl is afraid to release her completely.

The girl has good reason.

I must be out of my mind, she thinks. But is anyone in their right mind here? Certainly not her father or her brother and she has serious doubts about a mother who has gone along with all this— not only this woman in front of her but her sister and her own rape and pregnancy. Hiding her pregnancy. *When the time comes you'll go to Aunt Joan's,* she said. *No one need ever know.*

Insane. Stupid. Ms. Raton knew already.

So are you going to do this or not? she thinks.

Yes, you are. And damn the consequences. If she fucking kills you it might just be a relief.

She takes a deep breath and reaches up.

The Woman is free. She shakes her arms and hands which throb with pain as the heat of blood flows into them. The girl stands motionless before her like an animal in the wild that would wish to make itself invisible. But the girl is no animal in the wild. For a single moment the girl is able to meet her gaze.

***

Then the woman's hand darts suddenly out as though to punch or stab her in the belly—no, in the *womb*, in that most secret part of her, the part of her that has been violated by her father night after night, over and over so that she sees herself sobbing in her bed, sees herself sweating beneath him, and fearful that Darleen will wake she hears the bed creaking, she feels herself holding her breath against the smell of him, the stink of him, the woman's hand seeming to stab deep into the shame and pain that is her fertile womb.

And coming to rest there.

Gently moving, slowly. This is a caress.

Peggy can't help it, she begins to cry.

It's as though she's seen a miracle. *Felt* a miracle.

And she thinks, *maybe I have.*

"Oh my god, Peggy!" her mother says from behind her. "What in god's name have you done?"

Climbing painfully down the front steps she saw that the cellar door was open and she thought is that it? Is that who's doing all that screaming out there in the barn? Has Chris finally decided to feed the damn woman to the dogs? It's crazy but no crazier than anything else he's done lately. So she decided to check.

And now she stands at the top of the stairs and sees her daughter down there with her looking up at her as though dazed and the woman free of her chains and coming at her like a bullet from a gun.

This woman belongs to the man. She has stood by him as he hurt her with hot water and then with cold. She has hit her, held a gun to her head.

She takes the stairs three at a time and when she rams her shoulder into the woman's midsection, lifts her up and slams her down into the dirt she howls in pain. The Woman kneels and straddles her. She waves her arms trying to hit her or push her away and she bats them off like pests, like insects, like flies.

She is shaking her head and shouting. Her eyes are wide. The Woman digs her thumb and forefinger into those eyes and they pop like pits from ripe fruit and roll across her cheeks. She leans down and quickly bolts first one and then the other. Then her teeth find the soft flesh of her cheek.

The man's woman is no longer shouting now. She is making choking sounds as though it were she and not the Woman doing the eating.

The Woman chews, swallows, leans down and drinks from the sweet seep and spurt of blood. She turns the head beneath her hand, which offers no resistance—she has seen this many times before with the grievously wounded, it is almost like a kind of sleep—and bites deep into the other cheek.

She glances up as she chews and sees a thresher machine leaning against the side of the house, one of its blades propped upright beside it. She finishes chewing and sucks the blood from this cheek too. Then she hoists the woman up onto her shoulder and walks to the house.

She tosses her high up onto the steps. Hears her backbone crack against them and sees her head thump down like a log on a woodpile and loll off to one side.

She picks up the blade and runs her finger up and down.

It lacks a proper edge but it will do.

Peg hears her mother's shouts *Chris!Peg!please!help!help!* and then hears no more and even the dogs have abruptly stopped but it is as though she were tranced there standing in the cellar, she knows she should try to help her mother but she cannot, she's rooted there—and what she feels most strongly is a sense of *safety* though that makes no sense to her at all.

Safety. And calm. Though there's a wild woman loose. Safety.

Strange.

And then she thinks *god! Darleen!* and realizes her little sister's utter *lack* of safety—her vulnerability to everybody concerned dashes the calm, fills her with terror suddenly and breaks the spell.

She runs up the stairs and sees that the sun is setting, her house bathed in a warm yellow-orange light, sees her mother's broken body on the stairs in that same soft glow, steps over and around it and hurries inside, calling her sister's name.

Thirty-four

Cleek is rapt.

He has seen the dogs ravage a raccoon felled from a tree at night under the beams of his and his buddies' flashlights but never anything like this. Nor has he ever seen his daughter at work. If anything she's the most vicious of the four. She's digging teeth and bloody hands into the remains of the teacher's right breast all the way down to the exposed ribs. Agnes is at her side tearing into the woman's haunch while George and Lily have an arm and leg respectively chewed to the bone.

They're working as a team.

The teacher's face is gone. Her ears are gone. Her cunt and most of her ass are gone.

The dogs are sloppy eaters. There are bits of her scattered everywhere.

"Doesn't even look real anymore," Brian says, "does it, dad."

He's every bit as engaged as Cleek is.

"Does to me," he says.

He doesn't know particularly what he means by that but it has the ring of truth so he says it again.

"Does to me."

The barn door slams open and at first he doesn't believe what he's seeing. His mind is playing tricks on him. She's standing in the waning sunlight. There's blood smeared all along her face and neck and hands and staining Belle's baby blue dress. She's holding something a foot and a half long, wide and flat.

"Jesus wept," he says.

***

Peg glances out the window. Sees the woman striding across the yard toward the barn, taking her time, in no rush at all. *Moving away from the house, which is very good.* The woman's back is straight. There's an almost sensuous sway to her hips. Peg thinks of cats. Big golden cats.

She holds Darleen by the hand while with the other hand she's searching through the open drawer for a spare set of keys to the Escalade but all she finds are the spares to her mother's Toyota which are no good to her at all. The Toyota's at the shop. Her father's got the keys to the fucking Escalade in his pocket of course and there are no fucking spares in the drawer.

"Momma!" says Darleen. "I want momma!"

No you don't, she thinks. Not anymore.

You want me.

The Woman watches the man take an involuntary step back and go down stumbling in a shower of rakes and shovels. But the boy is frozen. Holding on to a dripping hose with his mouth open, staring at her. He looks like the stupid pig boy that he is.

The man is fallen so first it's the boy.

She crosses to him in three long strides and brings the weapon down into the soft flesh of his lower belly just above the hip and just beneath the rib. It's a practiced move. The boy shouts and drops the hose and leans instinctively into the bloody wound, grasping for it to stop the pain and the flow of blood and she tosses the blade into her other hand and brings it down on the corresponding side. The boy leans into that one too.

She tosses it again and strikes. Tosses a fourth time. Strikes again.

She is chopping him like a tree.

This tree is screeching now.

The man is trying to get to his feet so she rises up on one foot and kicks him back down amid the rakes and shovels.

Inside the cage the dogs are wild. Blood in the air. She can smell it too. Both inside the cage and out. It is the smell of conquest, of food, of life.

Twice more she tosses and strikes and on the second strike severs the spine.

The tree is felled—into two parts that drop away from each other.

And neither part knows that it is yet dead. The legs kick and tremble. The mouth and eyes open and close. The hands grapple with empty air.

Later perhaps she will eat of him. His penis perhaps. His nose. Perhaps the eyes that have watched her. But for now there is the man. Who is on his knees and reaching for something above.

Peg is going through Ms. Raton's purse looking for *her* car keys. She still has Darlin' by the hand but Darlin' is whining and crying, tugging at her, breaking her concentration. She dumps the contents of the purse on the living room floor.

"Goddammit, goddammit, goddammit!" she says.

They are either in her pocket or in the ignition. In either case she can't risk going outside to look. She can't risk having Darleen see her dead mother on the front steps either.

They're going to have to walk on out of there.

The Woman roars, steps over to the man and tears open the shoulder of the garment they've forced her to wear. It falls away from her and pools at her feet. She is free of all trappings of the man.

Cleek is in a panic but his hand fishes across the shelf and finds the stockless short-barrel twelve-gauge he keeps out there for varmints, a paper towel shoved in the end of the barrel against the dust and he brings it round. There is a moment of triumph as he swings it on her and *fucking bitch!* he shouts as the woman slaps the barrel up with the mower blade so that it's parallel to his head but he's already pulled the trigger. The towel shreds like snowfall all around him and he feels as though somebody's shoved an ice pick in his ear.

He falls to his knees again and drops the shotgun and both hands go to his blasted ear and the side of his head rough and bloody with buckshot and he looks up at the woman who is smiling.

Peg and Darlin' both hear the gun and Peg thinks, has her father shot her? Killed her? Can he somehow know that Peg is the one who set her free and is he coming for her next? For both of them? Her father is capable of anything, she knows that now. Darlin' is crying so hard she can barely get her breath. The poor thing's terrified. She needs a distraction. Anything.

Peg rushes her back into the kitchen. There's a six-pack of liter Deer Park water bottles on the shelf. She snatches one up and shoves it into Darlin's hands.

"Here. Don't drop this," she says. "Whatever you do, don't drop it. Let's go!"

It works. She's got something to occupy her mind now. *Don't drop the water bottle.* She's not choking on her own tears at least. She runs down the hall headed toward the front door.

"Wait! Stop!" Peg says. *Their mother's out there.*

Darlin' stops on a dime and turns to her.

"Back door," she says. "Come on."

The man is howling in pain. He raises a bloody hand to plead with her. Please! *he says. She understands that word. She has heard it many times before.*

She hacks at the man's wrist. There is not enough resistance and the blade isn't sharp enough to break cleanly through so the wrist hangs there by fragments of bone and tendon spouting blood. He raises the other hand to grasp at the first. She swings on that wrist too and the result this time is better. The hand tumbles through the air and clangs against the metal cage in which the dogs are barking.

No no no *he wails and she understands that word as well.*

He screams like a child as she lowers the blade.

She slices him open from crotch to sternum. For this soft flesh the blade is quite sharp enough.

The man looks perplexed it's so fast. The man doesn't know what's just happened. She shows him. She drops the blade and squats beside him and reaches to each side of the long wound and parts him as though the man were a stand of tall grass—pulls him open wide and buries her head inside him. Through the heat and wet of him she can hear him screaming.

She pulls out a length of intestine and spits it out immediately. The man's intestines are foul. The man is still conscious, waving his arms, looking down at her in defeat and horror. The hand has dropped off and lies beside him now. She dips her head inside him once again and bites down on his liver, pulls it out with her teeth and chews. The liver's foul too. She spits it out.

She reaches inside with her hand this time and wrenches out his heart.

And this she eats with pleasure. The heart is good.

She stands. The dogs have gone mad now, barking and clawing at the cage to get out, to get to two fresh piles of meat. There is also something very strange inside the cage. But this one is grasping *at the cage, not clawing at it. It has no eyes and it is as bloody as the rest of them. But this one is human. A human child.*

She remembers the voice she heard from inside the cellar. She hears it again now. Somewhere between a bark and a cry.

She goes to the cage and opens the door. The dogs rush out and fall upon the bodies. She sees that the dogs are not hungry—they've already fed—there's a third body mostly devoured inside the cage.

The dogs aren't hungry, they're angry.

The child rushes out too but the Woman grabs it by the back of the neck and hauls it up. She sees that the child is female. She struggles in the Woman's grasp and tries to bite. Socraigh, *she says,* socraigh. *Be calm. But the child will not be calm. She howls and snaps. The Woman slaps her, hard and only once, then strokes her. Strokes her head, her back, her shoulders and haunches. Her struggling slowly stops. She walks the child over to the man's body, stoops and retrieves his half-devoured heart and offers it to the child, who first sniffs at it and then grasps it and begins to eat.*

She stoops again and plucks out the boy's right eye and tosses it back into her mouth and chews. Let the dogs have the rest. There's a small child inside the house. Sighted, not like this one—and younger. She has seen her in the cellar with the rest of them.

The child will be tasty.

She scoops her weapon off the bloody dirt floor and walks out into the fallen night.

Thirty-five

Darlin's really scared again.

It's dark and they only have the one flashlight which keeps blinking on and off so that Peggy has to shake it to make it come on again and she doesn't know the woods at all—she's not allowed to play there. And where's momma? Why isn't momma here? And why's Peggy's hand so sweaty?

And what are they doing in the woods at night in the first place?

She's got the water bottle tucked under her other arm tight because Peggy said don't drop it whatever you do but then the light goes off again and her big sister's shaking it to get it to work and all of a sudden she's falling because her big sister's falling and she's going with her and the bottle gets away from her and Peggy says *ahhh!* and *shit! shit!* which she's not supposed to do.

The house is empty. She's knows that the moment she enters.

The Woman is amused. The child with no eyes has followed her and pads around her now on all fours panting like a dog as they make their way through the house. The child is very like her in a way. It can't see her but it can smell her. That sense has developed greatly.

Just as the Woman can smell the girl and her little sister. Their fear lingers in the air like the scent of a mud bank by a stream. They have gone out the back. When she crossed the yard to the barn she noticed that behind the house was all woodland.

They are in the woods. Standing on the porch her keen eyes discern a footpath and beyond that a trail.

They will be easy to follow.
Outside she bends into the light breeze and listens.

Peg's in a lot of pain. Her ankle's twisted badly. She knows this trail through the woods. It leads to a little stream and a mile or so after that, to Weber Road, which in turns leads out to the highway. She and Brian used to come down with empty Campbell's soup cans to catch crayfish in the stream when they were kids. But she's never been out here at night and with the goddamn flashlight on the blink there was no way to anticipate that hole she's just stepped into.

The flashlight's fallen from her hand but it's lying right beside her and ironically the jolt seems to have done it some good, its beam is steady now. She picks it up. Almost afraid that if she touches it the beam will disappear again but it holds.

She locates Darleen, who is in a panic, crawling around in the dirt trying to find her lost water bottle. She shines the beam across the trail.

"There it is," she whispers and holds the light steady on the bottle. Her sister crawls over and snatches it up and stands.

Peg needs to stand too but *damn!* it hurts to put any pressure on that ankle or even to move it at all.

But they've got to get out of here.

There's a sapling a few feet to her left just off the trail. She crawls to it on hands and knees and hauls herself up. Darlin's at her side trying to help. Of course she's no help at all. The beam skitters through the leaves of the trees above as she pulls herself up hand over hand and finally she's standing. Limping back onto the trail again. Every time she puts the foot down pain rockets through her leg all the way to the hip. She wonders if she's broken something. But she can't just hop. Not on this surface. She'd be down again in no time.

Suddenly Darlin' is standing stock-still in front of her.

She hears a twig break and then another and points the beam to where Darlin' seems to be looking. At the same time Darlin' raises the water bottle and holds it out in front of her as though the bottle were some sort of talisman to ward off evil.

Or an offering.

The beam falls on the woman. The dress is gone and she's naked now and covered with dried and drying blood which gleams in the light.

The woman. And scampering at her feet, her other sister.

The child has never known this kind of freedom. The child is beside herself with pleasure, shuffling at the feet of her liberator, taking in the rich scent of her and all the other countless scents she has never imagined and has no ability to name. Even the air smells wonderful and new.

But then she catches other scents and these she knows. She can even roughly calculate the distance between them and a scuffle of feet betrays their location exactly. These scents belong to her captors, two of them. They have not treated her badly. But they are one with those who do.

She growls and lunges.

The Woman slaps the child with the flat of her blade. She yelps and whimpers and backs away behind her, pacing nervously.

The Woman is curious about something.

The little girl is holding something out to her so she steps forward to see what it is. A bottle. Inside, water. The little girl she would spit over a fire and roast for dinner is offering her water. And unlike her sister she does not seem to be afraid.

The girl withdraws the bottle and struggles to open it and when it's open, holds it out to her again. This time she takes it and drinks deep.

She wonders what kind of girl this is. If she will understand something.

She lifts her left index finger and puts it to her mouth, sucks it and tastes the blood and when it's clean, shifts the bottle to that hand and holds out the right index finger to the little girl. The girl takes a step forward.

"Darlin'!" says her sister. From the way in which she says it the Woman suspects that is her name. Darlin'.

The little girl says something back to her sister and takes another step forward and touches the finger with her lips. The lips are closed and pursed. This is not sucking and it is not biting. This is just a touch.

Interesting.

Peg doesn't know what to think of all of this but that's her family's blood this woman is wearing, damned though they may be. Darleen's just a child, just an innocent, but what she's done repulses and confuses her. How can she possibly offer this person a kiss?

She hobbles painfully over to her sister and wraps her arms around her and then shifts her back so that Darlin's behind her and she's standing between the two of them. She's the one who let this woman free. It's her responsibility.

She knows what the woman can do. She doesn't yet know what *she* can do.

But something. Maybe.

Darlin's thought, the lady's hurt. She's hurt all over.

The lady needs a little kiss to make it better.

It's as simple as that.

"Please," Peg says, "just let us go."

The Woman holds out her finger again, this time to the sister.

"For the child, mother," she says. "For the child."

"Do ha leanbh, mathair," is what Peg hears. *"Do na leanbh."* The woman's voice is rough but not threatening. She understands, if not

what she says, what she's being asked to do. She's being asked to partake of blood.

She'll do no such thing.

The Woman's frustrated. Among her people this would be a gift, an honor. It would never be refused.

But her people are all gone.

Still, she thinks she knows what to do.

She approaches and the girl doesn't flinch at her approach. Her stance is rigid though. She's preparing to fight if necessary. The Woman could almost laugh at that but this isn't a time for laughter. A thought has occurred to her that she likes very much.

She reaches out just as she did in the cellar but slowly this time so as not to startle the girl as she would a wounded animal and rests her hand on her belly.

"Bah-bee," *she says.*

And there it is again.

That inexplicable sense of *safety* which is also a sense of being known, of being recognized, of simple acceptance that seems to emanate from this wild woman who kills and undoubtedly will kill again. And despite that fact she's comforted, she feels a burden lifted away unmixed with shame or guilt, a terrible huge relief.

She feels calmed. She feels free.

The woman seems to take her measure for a moment. Then she turns and walks off the path a few feet into the woods, bends down and begins hacking away at the limb of a birch tree. A few strokes is all it takes. She's amazed at this woman's power. The long hard muscles moving along her back. She forgets the blood and sees the power. She feels a strange kind of seduction going on here—as though the woman were dancing for her and her alone.

Is this what she could be one day? This strong?

Perhaps it is. *Is she wishing for this?* A part of her is, perhaps. A part of her is almost sure she is.

The woman returns to the path and hands her the limb. It will make a perfect staff to ease her wounded ankle.

She takes Darlin' by the hand and begins to walk away, leaving Peg alone there, her blind sister capering at the woman's heels. The woman's hips move side to side in a rhythm wholly unknown to her.

A few moments later, she follows.

The Woman has twice lost everything. Her parents' family and then her own. Her goods, her weapons. She has been scarred by knives and guns. She is naked but she will find clothing to her own liking as she always has. She will find other goods and weapons. The earth is a dangerous place for her, but it is also open to her. She can live in sunlight or in darkness as she chooses. She can eat of the creatures of the sea or of the land. The earth has a fist but it also has an open hand.

This night sky now—it belongs to her. Its dark will mask her. Its stars will guide her to the shore. She will find a cave and perhaps build a fire. She can hear the dogs behind her barking not very far away. The dogs will like a fire.

She has twice lost everything but the earth is rich with food and family.

COW

THE JOURNAL OF
DONALD FISCHER

October 2011
Somewhere near Canada, state of Maine

"She's going to do this, Donald," Peg told me. "There's no way I can stop her."

"Yes you can," I said. "She'll listen to you. She's *got* to listen to you."

I was desperate. I could hear it in my voice. I didn't like to hear it there. But propped up against the wall with my hands tied behind my back and my feet stretched out in front of me strung together at the ankles, and counting on what Peg had just told me was about to happen, you'd be desperate too.

Peg only smiled that sad lonely smile of hers.

"You haven't noticed? She knows what she wants. And she gets it."

"Is this because of today? Because if it is . . ."

"It's not because of today. It was what she planned on all along. It's not the first time."

"Jesus! Please! I can't *accept* this."

"Accept it, Donald."

"Some alternative. There's got to be some alternative."

She stood slowly and looked down at me and shook her head. The firelight flickered across her naked breasts, her naked thighs. Behind her the baby whined.

"You already know the alternative," she said.

***

Brother, be careful what you wish for.

I was wishing for community. Whatever *that* is.

I'm writing this now in a filthy battered spiral notebook with a Marriot Hotels and Resorts ballpoint pen, both of which Peg has provided me.

My hands are free for a change. And from now on, will be.

I have other shackles.

It may be that this is my last will and testament. Though I have nothing to will a soul. It may be I'll go crazy before I finish it. I don't know. Crazy or dead. It could be soon now. So I want to set this down.

Because either one is highly likely.

When they found me—us—we were on the beach rehearsing to the sound of incoming surf and high winds.

The play was one I'd written. A three-character one-act called *The Progerian*. It was set on just such a beach on just such a twilight evening, so the rehearsal was meant to feed my actors some inspiration. It was also a surprise. I'd told neither them nor any of the other cast or crew members about this. And it turned out just as I'd expected—they were delighted by the notion. The real-life equivalent of the drama's atmosphere.

I'd proposed we do my play as a sort of antidote to all that fucking Neil Simon. *Come Blow Your Horn* was okay though it got tired pretty quick but the entire cast hated *Barefoot in the Park* well before the opening-night curtain. And we still had *The Sunshine Boys* to get through before we sucker punched the entire Kennebunkport summer-stock area with Harold Pinter's *The Homecoming*.

We were all of us just a year graduated out of college either in Boston or New York and we were full of piss and vinegar. We had

ideals. We had enthusiasm and drive and love of the theater—
important theater—in common. With me as producer and director,
we considered ourselves a little community here.

I don't think we really knew the meaning of the word.

I do now.

Anyhow, we figured we'd do *Progerian* half price and run it
on Sunday afternoon only, an hour before *Barefoot*. Separate
admission.

We didn't expect much of an audience. It was abstract as hell
for one thing, a kind of cross between Pinter's stuff and Beckett's
Waiting for Godot, between which two writers I was more or less
stuck at the time. And since I'm not writing plays anymore I guess
I still am.

You know progeria? Most people don't. It's a rare malformation
of the ductless glands, which leads to premature aging of the heart,
the blood vessels and skin. By thirteen you're hairless and wrinkled.
By sixteen you look like a shrunken little old man. You're very lucky
to see your eighteenth birthday. In my play you're given to wry
enigmatic observations on the human condition. And why not? It
is, after all, a pretty unusual point of view.

Not unlike my own here.

It was early on in rehearsal. I think we'd only had two before this.
The actors were still on-book except for Linda, who had the fastest
line-retention skills I'd ever seen. So out of the four of us—with me
watching the three of them against the background of the sea—she
was the least distracted.

Linda was playing Honey and Sam was playing Butch, a not-
so-bright married couple with major problems who've come to
this romantic cliff by the sea to maybe patch things up by making
themselves a baby. *The family unit as Band-Aid, right?* Almost always
a bad idea. And an idea which running across this weird little guy
who declares he's sixteen but looks eighty can seriously mess with.

Especially when he says stuff like—and here I'm quoting from memory—"Rare though it is, the affliction reveals a mysterious presence within the human body, like a clock capable of running too fast or too slow, shortening life or extending it—and which is subject to evolutionary selection. A tail disappears, an opposable thumb is born, or a gene for aging. It becomes clear. We are alive by the grace of seconds only, subject to extinction in the wink of an eye."

Do I need to say they don't make the baby?

You're maybe wondering how I remember these lines so well.

It's not because I wrote them. At least not entirely.

It's because just as Art, my slim, delicate-featured progerian was finished reading them, that's when Linda pointed behind me and still in character as blowsy clueless Honey said, *"Who the* fuck *are they?"*

They were on us in seconds. A woman, a young girl, both of them stark naked—and at their heels something that bounded growling through the sand dunes like a skinned dog.

They say acting is *re*acting but the only one of us to react sensibly at all was Linda, who headed for the sea—directly *into* the sea. At just short of six feet tall and weighing in at about two hundred hard pounds Sam, I guess, decided to hold his ground. Art, who'd been staged sitting cross-legged on one of the dunes like some Zen master, tried to scramble to his feet.

I probably shouldn't have had that joint before rehearsal because all I had the sense to do was to try to duck before the woman hit me square in the forehead with the butt end of her knife and knocked me sprawling to the tide line.

She whirled on Sam—and standing his ground had been a mistake, because while he had the poundage and the muscle the woman was at least three inches taller than he was and she had the knife and she had reach. She came in low under his swing and then up and the next thing I knew the knife was deep in his throat slicing left to right and he was coughing blood and spurting blood all over her.

She took one glance back at me but it was clear I wasn't going anywhere. My legs had simply stopped working. I could barely feel them. Fear will do that to you.

Sam was still standing somehow so she put her mouth to his throat and her own throat started to work as she . . . swallowed him.

The girl had rushed past me into the water after Linda. Over the breakers I heard her shriek.

But it was the sounds coming from Art's sand dune that really got my attention.

The dog-thing was on him.

No, the dog-thing was all over him.

It was burly and squat but it was fast and biting him everywhere. The hands that tried to fend her off—I know it's a *her* by now—his arms, his legs, his cheek and he kept making these *eeee eeee eeee* noises like tires squealing on hot pavement, which broke finally into a huge hoarse howl when she simultaneously reached up and dug her fingers into his eyes and bit down into the crotch of his white cargo Bermudas.

By then Linda was stumbling back to shore sobbing and soaked head to toe with the girl right behind her and I couldn't help it, I noticed how erect her nipples were beneath the pale blue tank top, probably because I'd been checking out those breasts since the season started—but it looked as though the girl were simply *pushing* her and I couldn't think how that should be, how she wouldn't resist being pushed around by a teenage girl but then as they passed me lying there I saw the reason. The girl's knife was sunk into her back between the shoulder blades very near the spine. The girl had her hand wrapped around the hilt and was leading her along that way.

***

Peg later put it like this.

"We'd been scoping you out for at least half an hour from behind the dunes. Couldn't figure out what the hell you were doing at first and I don't think the Woman does to this day though I've tried to explain it to her. Anyhow we knew what we were after as soon as we saw you guys. And that's why you're still here and they aren't."

She paused a moment.

"Well, they are in a way," she said.

She has a nasty sense of humor, this girl.

I didn't see the rest because once Peg—the girl—pushed Linda face-first into the sand, she bent over and plucked a fist-size rock off the shallow water at the tide line and though I saw it coming there wasn't even a moment to *try* to duck this time because she was so fast swinging it at me. And I'm glad she did.

Because, as I say, I didn't see the rest of it, the actual kills.

She told me though. In the most matter-of-fact voice too. I'm sensitive to voices, to vocal nuance. The director in me.

It was like she was describing the events of a not-so-interesting day.

They began with Linda. Art was passed out and I was knocked out and Sam was *bleeding* out into the sand. So I guess Linda was the natural place to start. Even with that knife in her back the most likely to resist.

I'm going to try to remember every damn detail Peg told me here if I can. Just so you know. And I'm going to beg you not to stop reading no matter how rough this gets because I think it's important that you know.

I think it's important that you get to know Linda.

***

She was our lead, our ingenue. Funny, pretty and smart. And one tough lady too. Family out of Massachusetts. Strict catholic-school upbringing. So strict in fact that she'd trained in a novitiate to be a nun—the only actress I'd ever met or even *heard* of to take that weird circuitous route to her chosen profession.

Actresses by and large are not genteel, straight-laced or particularly religious people. They tend to cuss and drink like sailors and fuck like them too. They're perfectly willing to strip down naked in a crowded dressing room and are often called upon to entertain themselves and communicate to others the most blasphemous, frightening, radical, lewd, bawdy and free-spirited thoughts and words dreamed up by the people who write this stuff.

And this is what I mean by tough. Linda did all of that, with all the joie de vivre in the world. While her family sent her pious brother time and time again—even once to our cast house—to try to persuade her back to the fold. Back to the nunnery.

She'd have none of it. She was an actress born to the breed.

She also had a four-day-a-week workout habit.

The Woman pulled the knife out of her and handed it back to Peg. Then rolled her over. She was bending down to slit her throat when Linda heaved with her shoulders and threw her leg up sideways and landed her soaked Adidas solidly to the side of the Woman's head and while the Woman tried to regain her balance flipped over and was up and running down the beach.

Peg gave chase. But even wounded Linda was distancing her when the Woman shot past her like an Olympic sprinter and this time when the knife hit her back it neatly pierced and then severed her spine. The Woman rolled her over a second time.

She was paralyzed by then so I don't know how much she felt after that. If she felt them pull her clothes and shoes off, the salt spray and sea breeze on her naked body. If she saw them toss them into the sea. Peg thinks she didn't. Said her eyes were already glazed and staring. I don't know. But I guess they decided to be merciful at that point. I can only be glad they did.

"Maraigh ise," the Woman said. A kind of bastard Gaelic. Which translates, simply, to *kill her.*

So Peg did. Knelt on the sand beside her. Placed the knife between her breasts and with both hands, shoved.

They dragged her upright and slung her over the Woman's shoulder and then it was Art's turn.

Let me tell you about Art. About Art and Sam in fact.

They auditioned for us the same day and we hired them the same day, Sam based in Boston and Art in New York City. Turns out they'd been great friends since their senior high school play and no, they were *not* gay, thank you very much—not that this matters to theater people one way or the other—and they were having a ball working together again after all this time. Even if it *was* mostly Neil Simon thus far.

As a pair they were definitely Mutt and Jeff. As I said Sam was a big guy, serious-looking and good-looking, big baritone voice—your perfect lead. But he was versatile too. He'd played everything from the gentle narrator El Gallo in *The Fantastiks* to the sex-crazed Duperret in *Marat/Sade.* He was our uptight Paul Bratter in *Barefoot* and was set to play sleazy pimpish Lenny in *The Homecoming.*

Art was like a young Burgess Meredith. Always that mischievous twinkle in his eye. Always an ear for the pacing and punch line of a good joke. He was small and slight with already-thinning hair but he could morph into practically anything so long as it was funny. He'd been Sancho Panza in *La Mancha*, the husband in *The Fourposter*, Puck in *Midsummer Night's Dream.*

But they shared one bit of agony.

Art told me about it late one night, the two of us alone on the porch of the cast house under the stars, a half-shot bottle of Cutty resting between us on the floorboards.

"It's so damn mundane if it doesn't happen to you," he said. "Four college girls on their way to a party—they haven't even had a chance to have a drink yet for chrissake—slick road, wet leaves, hairpin turn, going just a little too fast. And then a tree. Did you know that the elm is the official Massachusetts state tree? You learn this shit sometimes when your sister drives into one.

"She met Sam through me, of course. They'd been lovers all the summer before. They were happy and hot as hell. She used to tell me how he'd Skype her naked when his roommate had gone to bed at night. She was one day ahead of him coming home from Amherst for spring break—their sophomore year. He'd forgotten to charge his cell phone so there was no way to get hold of him driving up from Philly so surprise, surprise, we hear his car in the driveway and he walks in grinning and his folks are there and I'm there and we tell him she's dead, Suzy's dead, my sister's dead, his lover's dead. Dead, dead, dead."

I remember he reached for the bottle.

"The elm tree is very resistant to splitting," he said. "Interlocking grain. They used it a lot for wheels. And coffins."

Who can judge and measure levels of human suffering? Which is worse, for your young son to die in war overseas or your young daughter simply to disappear one day, never to return? Is it worse to die wasted away in famine or in a hospital riddled with cancer? Agoraphobia or hypochondria? Which is worse? The hangman's noose or the headman's ax?

Beyond opting for a quick death or a lingering one who can possibly choose?

Between these two I know what I'd like. Probably you do too.

All that said, I think Art must have died hardest.

***

I've learned by now that the Woman has what passes in her world for a sense of humor. My first clue was when Peg told me what she'd named the dog-thing. *Soiceid.* Translation? *Socket.*

A girl-child, Peg's sister. Around eleven years old and born with anophthalmia. Born without eyes. Empty sockets where the eyes should be. Born in the dark, forever to live in the dark. The shame of Peg's family, locked away in a kennel for nearly ten years with the family coon dogs. Acting like a dog. *Thinking* like a dog.

And this is why I believe Art was the worst of them.

Because this dog was vicious.

I've already told you how she reached up and into Art's eyes maybe now you can understand the nature of that gesture. I've told you how she tore at his genitals, bit at his extremities, his cheek. But according to Peg when they reached him across the beach he was still very much alive. He was shaking his head *no* and what were left of his lips were trying to *form* the word *no* but he had barely any lips at all.

Socket had *kissed* them away.

"A kiss is a concealed bite," Peg told me. "I learned that from my father."

His cheeks were gone. His nose was gone. And Socket was gnawing on a long loop of intestine.

The Woman set Linda's body down beside him and Linda's left arm flopped into the cavity of his stomach. Then the Woman placed her knife between his bloodied teeth. He must have somehow recognized what this meant to him because he stopped the head-shaking and stopped his effort to speak. She set the knife at an upward angle and rammed it up through his soft palate into his brain.

This, for them I have learned, is mercy.

***

"Why me?" I asked her.

It was much later on. Long after I saw what they did to the bodies.

"Why them and not me?"

Peg only smiled. "You'll know soon enough," she said.

When tears are forced stinging from your eyes, when your throat is burning with acid, when your stomach is clenching and unclenching way beyond your control, when the dogs are barking, circling your vomit, racing from bloody carcass to bloody carcass across the rock face, you miss a few things.

But here's what I saw of Linda.

I saw them tie her to a tough narrow pitch pine by her ankles, her legs spread wide, her arms pegged to the ground, a naked human X—Linda X-ed out of the world, obscenely *crucified*—Linda, whose mouth hung open and whose eyes seemed to stare directly into me across the fire they'd built, accusing me of being alive.

I watched the Woman place her knife at the right corner of her jaw and make a deep ear-to-ear cut though her neck and larynx and the blood rush and then slow into the bucket beneath her head that little naked Darleen had brought to them from inside the cave behind me and Socket tentatively lapping from it, looking up at Peg as though to ask permission and that was when I began to vomit and draw the three big dogs' attention—unable even to wipe my chin because they'd tied my hands behind my back. Unable to move away from the stink of it because my ankles were tied too.

I saw Peg and the Woman massage her arms and legs in the direction of her torso and compress and release her stomach, draining her until the bleeding slowed to a trickle, then saw the Woman continue her cut from the jawline to the back of the skull slicing through muscle and ligament, gripping Linda's head on either side and twisting. I *heard* it break away from the spinal column. She set it on a rock and continued.

I didn't see the beginning of the skinning. By the time I looked up again they'd scored her flesh, dividing the surface of her body into dozens of squares and rectangles and were lifting and peeling with one hand while using their knives on the connective tissue beneath. They looked solemn, concentrated. I turned away again, saw Sam and Art on either side of me, the three dogs ravaging Art's body. Their muzzles glistening.

When I looked back Peg was flensing away a long strip of flesh from just above her navel to the base of her left breast and the Woman was on the other side, lifting a rough square of flesh off her thigh. Socket sat on her haunches, watching. Darleen was patting Socket's head. Feeding pieces of wood into the fire.

I'd thought I was done puking.

I'll spare you the rest of this.

Though they didn't spare me.

I'll spare you the gutting, the removal of the arms, the removal of the backbone, the halving and quartering, the removal of the ribs. The deep cuts along the calves and thighs and rump.

By the time they'd finished it was full dark beyond the flickering fire, beyond the pile of meat that was once a woman I'd admired.

And I was numb. Thankful to be numb and yet amazed to be numb.

I've since learned what you can get used to.

Sam was next. The pitch pine nearly couldn't manage him, sagging like a sad old man beneath his weight.

(*"How'd you get us up here?" I asked—again, much later. When I realized that sanity if there could be any lay only in talking.*

"Two trips." Peg shrugged.

"*How'd you get Sam up here?*"

"*She carried him. The Woman did. I carried you.*"

"You?"

"*We're a lot stronger than we look.*")

Then what was left of Art.

There wasn't much. Not after Socket and the dogs. The Woman didn't seem to mind.

"You'll want to eat this," Peg said.

She was handing me an entire sizzling steak skewered on a stick.

I told her she was out of her mind. That I could never.

She smiled. "That's how I felt at first. But hunger's what drives the bus. I said you'll *want* to eat this. Sooner or later, you will."

I told her she was disgusting.

"I can tell you all about disgusting," she said.

And then she did.

At first I couldn't even look at her.

There was grease on her face and hands and even though they'd gone down to the sea to bathe and were draped with skins against the chill night air I could still see smears and streaks of blood along what was exposed of their bodies, blood black beneath their fingernails.

There didn't seem to be anywhere inside the cave I *could* look without wanting to heave again. Certainly not at them eating by the fire at the mouth of the cave. Not at the second small smoke-fire at the back where they were drying strips of meat over some kind of tepee-style rack, strips that swayed in the updraft from the heat. Not at the stacks of raw meat, already buzzing with the few flies unmindful of the chill or at the huge battered stew pot beside them, filled with seawater to salt away what they did not intend to use more immediately.

My friends, it seemed, were everywhere. Scattered all around me.

But Peg wanted to talk. She seemed *starved* to talk and once she started there was no stopping her.

So I stared down into my lap and let her.

She told me about her father—and not once has she named the man to this day, he's always just *her father*—and what he did to the Woman and Peg and the rest of her family. How he captured the Woman when she was wounded and "off her game" as Peg put it and hid her chained in their fruit cellar ostensibly to "civilize" her but in fact to torture and molest her. A propensity for which he passed on to his son, who did likewise.

How he'd raped Peg nightly. Got her pregnant with the child Adam, who now squatted on the dirt floor of the cave with Peg's little sister Darleen, making clay shapes out of balls of mud. How he'd forced her to hide the pregnancy, to which her mother readily assented.

How he'd shut Socket away in the dog pen for nearly ten years.

I said little to any of this. I was looking for a way to play her. Some hint of empathy or sympathy that might get her to free me. I saw immediately that she was the only hope I had on that one. But I couldn't *figure* her. What in the hell was she doing here?

One look at the Woman and you saw she was a very seasoned hand at this. The scarring, the long tough musculature. The hard face. The wary watchful eyes. Then there was that strange guttural language. I hadn't heard her use a word of English—though later on I'd hear her use a word or phrase or two. But all of it combined now to make her distinctly *other*. As though she were almost a new species.

Or a very old one. Old as prehistory.

Peg was a different matter though. I'd seen her kill and I'd seen her butcher my friends, all without batting an eye. But I'd also seen her bend down smiling to accept a kiss and a hug from her little sister.

I'd seen her pick up baby Adam and bounce him up and down until he giggled and waved his hands in delight—just like any mother.

She'd spoken to me with civility. She'd done nothing unkind to me at all. It was hard to believe she'd abandon her own people so completely as to be here in this place.

It was the only card I could see to open with. So I asked her. *Why?*

"Look at her," she said. "Really, really look. She's magnificent. She's one of a kind. She's free. Free to be her own self by her own lights. Free of all restraint. You won't believe this now but she can be very kind. When she wants to be. And that's the key. *When she wants to.* There's no false *civilized* code of rules to follow. No phony politeness, no evasions. No lies. I don't think she even knows how to lie. She has courage, loyalty, generosity and power. She's the woman I want to be.

"I never knew that until the night my father murdered my teacher, who had only come to the house to talk openly with my parents about my pregnancy. My teacher, she had a lot of the same qualities. Courage, loyalty, generosity.

"What she didn't have was power."

I wanted to say, *this woman murders people. She butchers and eats them for chrissake!*

I was wise enough though to shut my mouth.

"They'll come looking for me," I said.

Peg nodded, gnawing on a bone.

"They already are out looking for you," she said. "We saw them two days ago. Half a dozen cops on the beach about a mile and a half down. Somewhere around noon. They'll give it up though."

"What makes you say that?"

"I know the currents here. Their clothes and your scripts are five or six miles away by now, most likely in deep water. And the beach itself? Sand doesn't give up many secrets. You sure you wouldn't like to eat?"

I starved myself for three days.

They brought me water when I asked for it and that was all, except to offer me the meat which I refused, which continued to turn my stomach every time I saw it or smelled it cooking. Mostly Darleen brought it to me.

But she never spoke to me. Not even when asked a direct question.

I knew she spoke. She spoke to Peg and to her baby nephew. She even spoke to the Woman. Often in the Woman's own language.

I asked Peg why not me.

"It's because you're a man," she said. "She may not show it particularly but you scare her, she's very unsure of you. She was terrorized that night, the night I set the Woman free. The night we ran away through the woods. The night my father and brother set Socket and the dogs on my teacher. And she knows who was responsible for all that fear because I told her. Her father and her big brother."

"*I* scare her? And the Woman *doesn't?*" She sure as hell scared me.

"Never. Not from the very first. She's pretty much got the language down too, after only about a year. She's much better at it than I am. Kids just learn faster, I guess."

Three days went by and still I wouldn't eat. The night of that third day the gnawing pain in my gut became a constant sense of pressure, as though someone had piled heavy rocks on my belly. I felt weak, faint. I could barely sleep. It was warm in the cave all day long and well into the evening but I shivered uncontrollably. My body temperature must have dropped by ten degrees. And then without knowing exactly when or why I found myself watching the pile of provisions slowly dwindle with an almost greedy sense of urgency. They were almost down to what they'd smoked or salted away.

The food was disappearing. I *had* to eat.

Each day Peg, Darleen and the Woman would go out to scavenge at the local dump leaving Socket and the dogs, *Agnes, George and Lily* behind to make sure I wasn't going anywhere and they'd return with what might have been useful to them but was totally useless to me—a filthy backpack, a broken saw, a cement-crusted wheelbarrow, bottles, cans, shoes, a toy for Darleen, somebody's old baby clothes. For Peg, a discarded book or two to read.

But they never scavenged for food and that's what *I* needed. The sea was just down the rock face. I could hear it all day long. It nagged at me. The sea was abundant with food—the kind of food I *could* eat. I begged Peg. A fish. A sea urchin. Seaweed. Anything.

You'll eat when you're hungry enough, she said.

And eventually, on the morning of the fourth day, I did.

A single strip of smoked meat. And then another. And another.

I kept it down too.

I thought about shipwrecks and longboats cast adrift, about the Donner Party and the Andes plane crash survivors. I was doing this to survive. I didn't want to die. That night when they roasted the salted rump steaks I ate that too. It was tough and stringy.

I *bolted* it down. And licked my fingers afterward.

I took an educated guess. Silently, I said my thanks to Sam.

It was understood that they'd broken me. The following day they returned to the cave with a wicker basket full of clams and a cardboard box at the bottom of which a dozen or so good-size blue-claw crabs scuttled over one another. They boiled it up for dinner.

They freed my hands and we had ourselves a good old-fashioned New England seafood feast.

Minus the drawn butter.

But after that it was back to salted or smoked meat.

"Why me?" I asked her. "Why them and not me?"

Peg only smiled. "You'll know soon enough," she said.

You've got to understand that I felt their eyes on me constantly. Not just the Woman and Peg but Darleen and little Adam too. I even felt Socket regarding me—sniffing at the air around me, cocking her head to listen if I made even the slightest move.

And as I watched our reserves of food deplete I began to wonder. Seriously wonder.

Was I their reserve supply? Was I simply *stockpile?*

Exactly why were they letting me live?

It was scaring the hell out of me and making me paranoid. Every time one of them would approach me I'd think, this is it, here it comes, here comes the knife. It was also making me angry. Fear and anger are kissing cousins I think. But I wasn't going to show that. If it was their intent to kill me any show of anger would only hasten the inevitable. Meantime I was still alive. And alive meant a chance at freedom.

But I had to know or at least get some kind of reaction. Something I could read.

I got no answers from Peg. So I decided to go to the head of the class. I'd ask the Woman.

Getting her attention was no problem at all. I already *had* her attention. She missed nothing going on in that cave. She was like some continually watchful animal, eyes darting everywhere, senses alert I think even as she slept.

Plus by then from listening to Peg and Darleen I thought I knew what to call her.

"*Be-an,*" I said. *Woman.*

I motioned with my head and arranged my face into an expression of request. *Come over here, please?*

She was sitting on a rock near the fire ring whittling to a sharp point a thin eight-inch length of bone. There were bones everywhere inside the cave stacked by length and size. You'd have thought they'd lived in there for months and not, as Peg told me, only for a matter of a couple of weeks. Some were human, that I knew firsthand. Most were not.

But there were more than just my friends' bones there.

She stood and set the knife down beside her and walked slowly over. Curious. She squatted down next to me and rolled the shard of bone between her thumb and forefinger.

They'd been tying my hands in front of me instead of in back since I started eating, only hauling them up over me tied to the head of a pickax they'd embedded in the rock when they were leaving the cave or going to sleep. But now they were resting in my lap. So now I pointed to my chest and said *me.*

She nodded. "Me. Yes."

It was the first English I'd heard her use.

I ran an invisible knife into my belly and dragged it upward. A mock evisceration.

"Kill me? Yes?"

She smiled. Peg had a pretty smile. The Woman did not.

"No," she said.

The relief was enormous. I believed her. I would have even if Peg hadn't told me she didn't know how to lie. But I still couldn't understand.

"What, then?" I asked.

The Woman stood and shrugged. Looked me over for a moment

from head to toe. My filthy clothes. My black-stained unwashed hands.

And then went back to her whittling.

"What are you reading?"

It was late, the fire just a dim flickering glow, and Peg and I were the only ones awake.

The book was a dirty old paperback with no cover.

"*Siddhartha*," she said. "Hermann Hesse. Ever read it?"

"Yes. Back in college."

"I like it. *'I can think. I can fast. I can wait.'* I like that. I like that very much."

On the morning of the seventh day I awoke to raised voices. They were arguing. Peg and the Woman. Circling each other around the dead ashes of the fire like a pair of wrestlers about to come to grips, pointing at each other and gesticulating wildly, shaking their heads. While the dogs and Socket cowered in a corner and Darleen looked on with a kind of placid interest.

At first I had no inkling as to what the hell it was all about. Apart from the occasional *no no no!* from Peg it was all in the Woman's language. But Peg was acting very strangely, that much I could tell, very out of character.

She was . . . *petulant.* Pouty. She actually stamped her foot at one point like the teenage kid that I guess she was. Though you'd hardly have known it. To the contrary, her behavior around me at least had always been adult way beyond her years.

But this was a kid throwing a small tantrum here.

Her voice was up an octave.

It took me a few minutes to realize that I was included. Despite the glances in my direction. That in some way the argument was about me. Which completely confused me. I couldn't figure why that should be. What did I have to do with anything? I was just their captive here.

But when the Woman pointed at me and roared *tu dheanamh!* there was no question. I was involved all right.

And Peg looked utterly defeated. As though the Woman had struck her. Her face broke. For a moment I thought she was about to cry. Then she turned and raced out of the cave.

The Woman—calm now, the storm passing as quickly as a gust of wind—simply looked at me and nodded.

We were walking down the far side of the cliff, away from the sea. A path through the scrub.

"Tu dheanamh," I asked her. "What does it mean."

"You do it," she said. "It was a command." She'd thoroughly regained her composure.

"Do what?"

"You'll know in a little while now."

An hour or so later when Peg returned it was as though the argument had never happened at all. There was a brief conversation between the two of them and Darleen and then they each began dressing in the clothing they'd collected from the dumps or stolen off clotheslines and they did so in total silence while Socket and the dogs sat eagerly waiting.

Then Peg walked over to me.

"Come on," she said. "We're going to clean you up."

"We're going outside?"

"Yes. Get up."

"Outside where?"

"There's a stream. A pool. You going to make trouble? Are we going to have to carry you?" She untied my legs.

"No. Hell, no."

204 JACK KETCHUM & LUCKY MCKEE

I hadn't washed in a week. You don't know how much you miss that daily shower until it's denied you. I smelled worse than the dogs—who'd at least had the occasional dip into the sea.

The Woman was already dressed and waiting at the mouth of the cave. Shorts and a plain black T-shirt. Peg's said MYSTIC SEAPORT and Darleen's said ODYSSEY FANTASY WRITING WORKSHOP 2009 on the front and SIXTEEN STRANGE TOADS IN A STRANGE GARDEN on the back.

You had to wonder where they'd got that one.

We walked uphill along a slate and gravel path to the top of the cliff which in turn led to another path downhill through scrub and high grass, the dogs and Socket leading the way. I walked squinting into the unaccustomed sunlight with Peg just behind Darleen carrying little Adam, the Woman behind me.

I wasn't about to run for any number of reasons. It was clear to me that they knew this terrain far better than I did for one thing, and I wasn't too sturdy on my legs after a week of hardly using them for another. Finally, Peg and the Woman each wore belts. And in each of those belts was a very sharp knife.

I heard the stream long before I saw it. A *fresh* sound. A *clean* sound. Much different from the constant splash and boom of surf. It was as though the ocean were somehow contained, static, buffeted against a wall of earth while the stream ran free.

"Can we stop a minute?" I said. "Is that okay?"

"Why?"

"The, uh, running water?"

Peg looked at me a moment and then laughed.

"You have to pee. Sure, go ahead. Not too far though."

She shouted something in that language of theirs and Socket turned and the dogs turned and waited while I stumbled off a little ways into the scrub and indulged in—as my uncle used to say—*the pause that refreshes.* And that felt free too, after a week of pissing and shitting into a chipped porcelain bowl. Aside from the fact that my hands were tied it almost felt *normal.*

"Why the clothes?" I asked her once we started walking again. "You usually go without, right?"

"Just a small precaution. From a distance, what do we look like? Clothed, I mean. A family out for a walk through the woods, that's all."

"But if they get anywhere near up close . . ."

"If they get anywhere near up close that's their problem."

She's awfully sure of herself, I thought. There could be hunters out here. People with guns. I asked her about guns.

"We've used them," she said. "The Woman can hunt with anything, including a shotgun or a rifle. But they're too damn noisy. And then there's the problem of ammunition. We can't very well just waltz into a gun shop and ask for a box of twelve-gauge, can we."

"You could."

She smiled. "No ID. Not anymore."

"And hunters don't worry you?"

"My father was a hunter. She killed him. Said his guts were all over the barn."

"Strip," she said.

I was more than willing to do that by then. The morning was heating up and my clothes were sticking to me like dirty, smelly masking tape.

The dogs and Socket were the first ones in but the pool was wide and deep beneath the cascade of water from the stream above and there was plenty of room for all of us. The dogs didn't stay long—just paddled in circles for a while and then raced up the rocks shaking themselves to lie down snorting in the sun.

Socket seemed to like the water though and for a while all five of us were in there, little Adam happily splashing close to the shoreline.

The water was very cold initially but felt wonderful running slowly over my skin to tumble down to more granite rocks below and in a while you got used to the cold. Peg passed me a half-used bar of coarse soap and watched me while I washed my hair, my face and hands and then, turning away from her in some futile attempt at modesty that I knew even then to be ridiculous, the rest of me.

I passed it back to her when I was through and just bobbed there awhile enjoying the sensation.

It struck me though. Scrubbed clean, Peg seemed like almost a different person. Like a normal young girl. And a pretty girl at that. It wasn't that I was noticing this for the first time. She was almost always as naked in the cave as she was now. Her body was slim and tight, particularly her ass and thighs. Her breasts were small, with long pointed nipples, her pubic hair a light brown, almost blonde, unlike the long, much darker hair that now shone dripping in the sunlight.

As I say, I'd noticed all this before. Of course I had. I'm a man. Just as I'd noticed the Woman's lithe powerful body. But it was the first time I hadn't had very mixed feelings about noticing. It was the first time I wasn't viewing her as some kind of educated savage.

She went about her business quickly and efficiently and then tossed the bar of soap to the Woman across the pool from us who caught it handily, sniffed at it and made a face. Which made both of them laugh.

So she can laugh, I thought. *The Woman can laugh.*

When she was finished—a cursory job compared to mine and Peg's, you could tell she really didn't like doing this much—the Woman handed the soap to Darleen, who splashed over to Socket doggy-paddling beside her and washed her first and then herself. Socket seemed to like the attention. Then she walked over and soaped up Adam, who immediately began to cry. She didn't let that bother her.

"*Out,*" the Woman said when Darleen was through and clapped her hands once.

Her face had gone serious and stern again. We listened.

Climbing out of the pool I turned to Peg.

"Can I do my clothes? They reek."

"Why not," she said.

She said something to the Woman and the Woman shrugged and said something to Darleen and Darleen handed me the soap. Then they all sat and watched me at the water's edge scrubbing and rinsing out shirt, pants, briefs and socks, wringing them out as dry as possible and putting them on again. The sun was high by the time I'd finished.

It was the best I'd felt in a week. I felt *human* again.

It wasn't about to last.

"Hands behind your back," she said.

"Why?"

"Just do it."

She'd only just untied them and I'd wondered why. Now I knew. She was going to *re*tie them. I didn't like it.

"I don't get it. I've done nothing. I'm eating . . ."

"Just do it, *Donald.*"

Whenever she used my name I knew it was serious. I was propped up against the wall of the cave again on my browse-bed. My feet were tied together again. My little journey into the great outdoors just a memory. A dream of freedom. Of something approaching normalcy.

We'd eaten. This time it was dog. God knows where the Woman got it from. Stolen or trapped. I'd learned that they had traps set all throughout the woodlands. Traps for rabbits, squirrels and bigger game. But I know a dog when I see one skinned or not. This one was about the size of a Labrador. Agnes, George and Lily were still at the bloody carcass. So the dogs were cannibals too.

I did as she said.

I was aware that the others, the Woman and Darleen and even Adam on her lap were all watching me with interest. Watching us. Silent, sitting around the fire. Socket was dozing at the Woman's feet.

When she was done Peg sat back on her haunches and looked at me and sighed. She looked over her shoulder at the Woman, who just stared at us unblinking and then back to me again.

"What?" I said.

She reached over and unzipped my pants and parted my briefs and drew my cock out with her long slim fingers.

I was too stunned at first to say a thing.

She started working my cock with both hands. Up and down and side to side. I realized she'd greased them.

"Why . . . why are you doing this?" I said.

She smiled. It wasn't a good smile.

"Don't you like it?"

"I . . ."

"I'm ovulating," she said. "You're going to make a baby. Hopefully a male baby. Adam needs a baby brother. We need males. You asked *why me? This* is why you."

I glanced up at the Woman, at Darleen and Adam.

"This is crazy. This isn't going to work," I said. "Not with them there."

"It'll work," she said. *"I learned it from my father."*

It took a while but she was right.

I closed my eyes against the three of them watching me and only opened them when she climbed on top of me and even then stared only at her—at her hard concentrated eyes and open mouth, the clean brightness and the long sway of hair, at the sweat gleaming across her breasts and belly, the straining muscles of her arms and thighs.

There had been no one in the cast I'd had sex with. I hadn't touched myself in maybe a month.

When I came it took my breath away.

Twice more that night.

In the morning just before first light she came to me again. The others were asleep. I could hear the Woman snoring. Even in the dim gray light I could see the determined grim set to her jaw as she moved her hand on me. This was not about me and not even about her when you got down to it. This was about that day-and-a-half window of fertility.

"You really don't like doing this, do you," I said.

"Would you? If you were me? You know my goddamn story."

"Untie me. Untie my hands, my legs. I won't try to run. I swear."

"Why should I?"

"Let me try something. Just once."

I was playing her and maybe she saw that. But a part of me simply wanted to do this too.

"I don't think so," she said.

"Untie me. Let me take off my clothes. Did your father take off his clothes? He didn't, did he."

I was guessing from what she'd told me that he wouldn't have dared, the sick bastard. Not with Darleen asleep in the next bed right beside them. Not with his wife just down the hall.

"No," she said.

"Okay. So let me touch you."

"*He* touched me."

"Not that way. Not in the way you're thinking. Let me try. What have you got to lose, Peg?"

For a few moments she just sat there thinking. Exactly what she was thinking I'll never know. But then she made her decision and reached over and untied the rope around my legs. I leaned forward so she could free my wrists as well.

"Thank you," I said.

"Now what?" she said.

"Come here. Lie down next to me."

I held out my arms. She hesitated. Shook her head.

"I don't know about this," she said.

I waited. Slowly she eased herself down. Her head against my chest. Her hands balled into fists tucked up tight under her chin. *Relax,* I told her and just held her awhile until finally her hands did relax and I could feel her heartbeat and breathing return to something that didn't feel like the flutter of trapped birds against me.

I kissed the top of her head, her forehead.

"Don't do that," she said. "He did that."

"Tell me something," I said. "Were you always clothed when he came to you at night?"

"I was always in my pj's, yeah."

"So he never did this, did he?"

I slid down her body and kissed her naked shoulder, her collarbone, the top of her breast. I was slow and I was gentle. Still I could feel her tense. I slid down farther past her breast and kissed her along her side, her waist, along her belly to her navel.

"What are you doing?" she said.

"I'm making love to you."

"You are, huh?"

"That's right. You got a problem with that?"

She laughed.

"So you're my lover now, is that it?"

"That's right."

"You're an ass."

"That's right. I'm your lover and I'm an ass. Come here."

I pulled her tighter to me. She didn't resist. And a moment later I could feel her hands rest lightly on my back. They didn't move but they were there.

I moved slowly up from her navel to her breast and rested my cheek there. I could feel her nipple tighten and rise beneath it. I turned my head and kissed her there and kissed her again. Then I opened my mouth and took the nipple in.

Oh, she said. A tiny sound of surprise. I used my tongue and then gently, my teeth—and her hands began to move across my back and shoulders down over my waist to the crack of my ass. She was exploring me. I'd never made love to a virgin but that's what this felt like. That's what *she* felt like touching me. As though I were altogether new.

And that emboldened me.

I drew myself down over her body and parted her thighs. I'm not sure she knew what I was up to at first but then she did.

Wait! she said but I didn't wait. I buried my face in her. I parted the lips of her cunt with my tongue and found her clitoris a moment later and worked it round and round and heard her grunt and felt her hands on my head pushing me away but her heart wasn't in it, she was stronger than I was so she could have but she gave in to it instead, she let her hands rest on the back of my head and soon I heard her moan and she began to buck. I gripped her ass tight between my hands and finally I could feel her flush and she shuddered and bucked one last time and when I pulled away and slid my cock inside her my face was bathed in her and her cunt was slick and warm as it had never been before.

When I rolled off her body and lay down beside her I heard a kind of *snicking* sound coming from the direction of the fire. I glanced over. There was the Woman—wide-awake and whittling another length of stark white bone.

Watching us.

***

Peg never returned to me after that morning. Her ovulation was over.

In fact she barely spoke to me over the next day or so. It was as though what had passed between us embarrassed her and perhaps it did. Or perhaps she too knew that the Woman had been watching.

We lived the next couple of weeks on the fruits of the land, the stream and of the sea. Stewed lean beaver meat. Rabbit. Raccoon brined overnight, parboiled and roasted. Trout from the stream. Crabs, clams and mussels. Blueberries, blackberries. Boiled dandelion, ostrich fern, pigweed, cattail, wild onion. Leached acorns. Water lilies and seaweed. They'd found an apple orchard. So we ate a lot of apples. We were never hungry.

When Peg was speaking to me again I asked her—*why, then, with all this plenty, did they hunt humans?*

"She tried to explain it to me once," she said. "She said something like, the best food understands its own death, its sacrifice. And the deeper the understanding the more that supports the living. She said that all life understands the passing of life, down to the smallest insect, the smallest flower. That it's only a matter of degree. And that's why we eat the flesh of our own. More than any other creature, we have understanding."

"So you're telling me it's spiritual. A spiritual thing."

She shrugged. "Whatever. I dunno, maybe. Maybe it is."

They were out late one night, leaving me alone with Darleen, the dogs and baby Adam. All of whom were sleeping. I couldn't sleep. The idea that if I could free myself from these ropes, from this pickax over my head and quietly tiptoe out of there was keeping me awake. As it had many nights before.

But that was impossible. The dogs were there. The dogs were alert to the slightest movement. And it was the dogs pricking up their ears that alerted me to their return. Long before I heard the muffled screaming.

It was a woman or a young girl. I couldn't tell exactly which at the time though from the pitch of her voice I was betting on the young girl. And later I'd learn that I was right. A teenager. Snatched off the roadside when her car broke down.

Her very bad luck that night.

But I could imagine her. Strung up from that pine tree just like Linda. Screaming for mercy. Screaming in fear. Naked and crucified upside down in the flickering firelight.

More than any other creature, we have understanding.

And then a sudden silence.

In that silence I imagined the flick of the blade across her throat, the rush of blood into the bucket spilling across the Woman's hands or Peg's hands, the cross-hatching of her flesh, the careful peeling away of that flesh, the severing of sinew, ligaments, fascia, the crack of bone, the rasp of the knife. I imagined the severed head, the fixed eyes, the mouth open as though in wonder.

I could almost hear her last thoughts clearly in my mind. *Can this be happening to me? To* me? *Is this possible?*

They set up the smoke-fire and replenished our stocks.

Blood has an iron or copper smell when it's fresh and the cave now reeked of it. Iron and smoke.

So did they.

Which meant that when the Woman squatted beside me and set the bowl of blood in front of me I nearly gagged at her proximity. Her hands and forearms were caked with it and there was splatter all across her face and breasts and belly and all down her legs.

She grinned at me. Her teeth were not a fine thing to behold.

And then she did as Peg had done—though she did it far more

roughly and with far more intent. Reached over and freed my cock from my pants and briefs. I shook my head.

"No," I said. "No way. No way in hell."

Peg was stoking the fire near the mouth of the cave and she was grinning too.

"It's her time of the month," she said. "Enjoy."

The Woman dipped her hand into the bowl and began to stroke me slick with fresh blood.

"Please," I said. "Don't do this."

She dipped her hand again. There was blood all over me now.

I tried to will it away. To will myself not to rise. But she was expert at this. Teasing the glans with her fingertips, stroking in half circles, teasing again. Dipping her hand and stroking. Expert too at reading me. At reading when I was about to come.

When she knew I was ready she straddled my body with her back to me and lowered herself down and I could see the muscles of her shoulders, back and thighs rippling in the shadows and then I was coming and angry at being made to come so that I pounded at her, trying to hurt her, tear her open—but she matched my every stroke with a force equal to my own so that I was the one hurting, my hips, my thighs, my ass chafing against the browse-bed.

I was trying to rape but I was being raped myself.

"God *damn* you!" I screamed.

She sat there a moment. I was breathing as though I'd run a four-mile race. Her own breathing was slow and steady. She lifted herself off me and without even once looking back at me walked over to help Peg feed the flames.

The second time, later in the night, she freed my hands and once I was hard, got down on all fours, presented her ass and cunt to me.

"No," I said. "No."

She turned and glared at me and growled. *"Tu dheanamh,"* she said.

I knew what that meant. *"You do it."*

So I did.

And that morning in full view of all of them, did it again.

It came to me that this was what I was. This was what I descended to. I was owned. Property. Livestock.

A cow. I was a cow.

To be milked and milked again.

I couldn't help my resentment and I couldn't hide it either. However irrational under the circumstances, I felt that Peg had betrayed me.

"Who's next, Peg?" I said. "Socket? Darleen?"

"Don't be ridiculous," she said. "Darleen hasn't got her period yet. Silly."

"We're moving."

It was first light and the cave was all activity—the Woman, Peg and Darleen dressed in jeans and T-shirts stuffing old backpacks with clothes and pots and pans and toys for Adam, piling the wheelbarrow and a rusted once-red wagon with tools and weapons while the dogs and Socket circled eagerly around them.

"Why?" I said. "Where to?"

"We've taken four people here. Five, if we count you. And one not far away before you. We make it a point not to stick around in any one place too long. People get missed. There's a place inland four or five miles away upstream from where we swam that day. Somebody probably built it as a hunter's cabin years ago but the land's all swampy now. The place is abandoned."

She nodded toward the Woman.

"She found it last week and I went to look it over yesterday. It'll do for a while."

"It's in a swamp?"

I was thinking *mosquitoes, snakes.* I had misery enough.

"The edge of a swamp. You'll see."

When they were ready the Woman untied my feet and the knot binding me to the pickax. Wrenched it out of the rock and tossed it onto the wheelbarrow.

"Bog," she said. *Move.*

In her belt, flanked by the two sharp shards of bone I'd seen her whittling, the big knife gleamed in the morning light. I wasn't about to argue with her.

Our column to the stream was the same as before—Socket and the dogs out front, then Darleen and Adam followed by Peg and me and the Woman right behind us. Once there we followed a narrow dirt path that wound along its western border. You couldn't see much of the stream except for a few glimpses of it glittering through the trees but you could hear it all the way and that was quite enough to make me yearn for a good cold bath. To rid myself of the stink of blood and wood smoke I carried around with me like some noxious cloud.

Peg seemed to read my thoughts.

"We'll clean up once we're there," she said.

The sun was hot and high by the time we reached the cabin. Socket and the coon dogs were panting. The rest of us were drenched with sweat. If we stank before, we positively reeked now. I could imagine deer, rabbits, squirrels, every animal in the woods hightailing it anywhere but in our direction.

The cabin stood alone in the middle of nowhere. Along one side the stream ran shallow and clear. Along the other, pooling out from what had once been the front door, it had diverted into swamp water two or three inches deep and extended through the forest, the cattails and swamp grass, as far as the eye could see. Through this nasty muck we slogged to the cabin, which must have been well over a hundred years old, sturdily built out of cut logs but spongy now to the touch.

The windows and doorway were open to the elements but the roof was still intact. Strong hand-hewn beams. If somebody had bothered to drain the swamp fifty years ago they might have had a nice little place here. That and killed off the mosquitoes.

I was slapping at them like crazy.

"Woodsman's dope," Peg said. "We'll wash up and then put some on. Keeps *everything* at bay. Mosquitoes, black flies, deer flies. You think the mosquitoes are bad? Those flies can be hell in season. They'll bite you bloody. She makes the stuff herself. Pine tar, camphor, citronella, bunch of other shit."

They cut some pine boughs and swept the place. Mouse droppings and rabbit turds. Beetles. The desiccated corpses of grasshoppers. A small colony of red ants feeding on a broken-necked sparrow in the narrow stone fireplace.

I helped them lay our browse-beds. The dogs were off chasing something—we could hear them barking upstream—and Socket flopped down with a snuffle and a deep sigh. Uncanny though her senses were—eyeless, she could somehow manage to avoid any rock or tree in her path—she was still too slow to join them.

An hour later we were naked in the brook. Unlike the place downstream there were no deep pools here. At best there was only five inches of water down to the pebbled bottom so that you had to either sit or kneel in it, use the soap and splash yourself clean.

And that was what the Woman was doing when I saw my chance.

The stream ran narrow here and turned to a U-shape along the eastern bank where I'd seen a second dirt footpath through the lush ferns just across from us. Not far from me, on our side, was a stand of slender white birches hanging low over the water, mirrored by a second stand amid the ferns. It wasn't hard to inch my way over to the trees on my side, which offered partial concealment.

Just doing this much, my heart was pounding.

Peg was busy turning over rocks, catching crayfish in her hands and dumping them into an empty pickle jar. A snack for later on. Darleen had her back to me, washing Adam's hair. Socket was sound asleep on the shore.

The dogs still hadn't returned.

So that when I saw the Woman, sitting, lower her head to the water to splash her face I made my move. I quietly slipped to the birches on the far side of the stream. Moved up the embankment into the ferns and from the ferns onto the path.

And then I was running faster than I'd ever run in my life.

Never mind that I was naked. Never mind that brambles and tree branches seemed to lunge at me out of nowhere. Never mind the beating my bare feet were taking along that rough pebble-strewn path. *I was fucking running. I was free.* I was bursting with adrenaline and some manic determined joy.

I leaped over rocks and rammed my way through scrub.

Ahead of me to my right I could see a high field of goldenrod and behind that, dense forest. *That would be my goal, that forest.* I'd get lost in there. I'd wander around lost until I found someone or someone found me. I'd tremble at night with the cold. I'd starve. I'd go thirsty. *Anything.*

She appeared directly in front of me not ten feet away. Dripping wet from the stream.

"Is leor sin!" she said. And then in English, *"Enough!"*

She wasn't even breathing hard. She walked over. Her eyes looked calm, blank, empty. I saw no malice there.

But the knife was pointed directly at my cock.

I heard Peg come up behind me.

"You had to try, I guess," she said. "Sooner or later. I know I would have if I were you."

I felt the point of her own knife in the small of my back.

"But I'm not you," she said. "Am I?"

In the late-afternoon sunlight the Woman sat in the empty doorway. Whittling bone.

"She's going to do this, Donald," Peg told me. "There's no way I can stop her."

"Yes you can," I said. "She'll listen to you. She's got to listen to you."

I was desperate. I could hear it in my voice. I didn't like to hear it there. But propped up against the wall with my hands tied behind my back and my feet stretched out in front of me strung together at the ankles, and counting on what Peg had just told me was about to happen, you'd be desperate too.

Peg only smiled that sad lonely smile of hers.

"You haven't noticed? She knows what she wants and she gets it."

"Is this because of today? Because if it is . . ."

"It's not because of today. It was what she planned on doing all along. It's not the first time."

"Jesus! Please! I can't accept this."

"Accept it, Donald."

"Some alternative. There's got to be some alternative."

She stood slowly and looked down at me and shook her head. The firelight flickered across her naked breasts, her naked thighs. Behind her the baby whined.

"You already know the alternative," she said.

Long after it was over I was lying by the fire in the old stone fireplace and Peg was tending to my wounds when Darleen stepped over to us and squatted down beside me—looked me straight in the eye. Which she had never done before.

"You're not mean," she said. "Are you."

"No," I said. "I'm not mean."

I could barely speak. It came out as a whisper.

"My daddy was mean," she said. *"E scanraigh me."*

"In English, Darleen," said Peg.

"He scared me," she said. Her eyes were wide. Perhaps she was remembering. "But you're not mean. No."

And then she did the most astonishing thing.

She leaned over and gently kissed my forehead.

I will never fear pain again, I think.

I've been to the mountain.

With the Woman's arms around me it was useless to struggle and would have been even had my hands not been tied behind my back, my ankles bound together and besides, it would have only ripped my flesh open further. So that when Peg pressed the first long shard of bone deep into the muscle between the nipple and the collarbone of my left breast, worked it through the tough muscle and drew out the other side I screamed and howled behind gritted teeth and waited for it to be over, to be mercifully swift, for the burning pain and the invasion, the *movement,* to stop inside me.

And Peg didn't linger at the task. I could see she took no delight in this. It was duty and duty only, concentrated and steady. She gave me a moment to breathe, to relax slightly in the Woman's arms, for the muscles in my breast to stop shuddering, quivering. Then she pushed the second bone through my right breast too.

The third bone was smaller. But equally as sharp.

They laid me down on my back on the browse-bed. The Woman raised and held my legs in the air directly above my head.

I knew what this was going to be. Peg had told me. I was already trembling.

"*Faoi shiochain,*" the Woman said. *Be at peace.*

And then Peg carefully drew the third bone through the base of my scrotum.

It's been about four months now.

The events I've written about took place in July. Now, by my reckoning, it's October, somewhere around Halloween. But there won't be any trick-or-treaters coming around here. We've found another abandoned house in the woods up here not far from the sea. I remember from my former life that the economy was hitting everybody pretty hard and I guess that hasn't changed. It's a good house. Only a couple of years now gone to seed, I'd say. It'll shield us from the weather. Peg says we're almost to the Canadian border.

They led me here by a pair of tethers, one looped around each of the horizontal bones in my chest.

Livestock remember?

The third bone's for a different purpose.

It's true what they say about genital piercings.

It makes me a more efficient cow.

But what I said about pain is also true. I'll never fear it again. I swear I'll tear these bones out of me with my bare hands if given the slightest chance at rescue. One hunter with a gun. One scout troop traipsing through the woods. One car close enough on the open road ahead of us at night.

There's an old battered desk here and I'm leaving this in a drawer just in case I die or do go mad before then.

Because Darleen, little Darleen, had her first period the day before yesterday.

And god help me, I'm the cow.

CPSIA information can be obtained at www.ICGtesting.com

260021BV00001B/2/P